Praise for

Feeding the Enemy

"JR Sharp, in his novel, *Feeding the Enemy* , artfully blends, in the rich tradition of oral history, his family's most intimate recollections of living under the grip of fascism with a highly accessible chronicle of the brutality and devastation of World War II. His skill and flexibility as a storyteller is revealed in this historiographical narrative that boldly recounts events in a small northern Italian village from the one true perspective, that of the common man. His people's history point of view counters the conservative, elite polemic that dominates history while enfranchising the personal bonds of family to the past. History from below at its finest."

—Dr. Alan S. Canestrari, Professor of History Education, Roger Williams University, Bristol, RI

"Feeding the Enemy is a fascinating family saga of undying love, personal sacrifice, quiet heroism, and triumph. Using untold hours of oral family history, personal interviews, and exhaustive research, author J.R. Sharp skillfully records the trials and tribulations of the Zucchet and Cartelli families and their struggle to survive the horrors of Nazi occupation and brutality during World War II Italy. You don't want to miss this "You were there!" story!"

—E. Michael Helms, author of *The Proud Bastards, Of Blood and Brothers,* the *Mac McClellan Mystery* series, and others.

"Feeding The Enemy by J.R. Sharp is a brilliant book and one of the most powerful stories of survival I have ever read. An essential piece of WWII literature and a must read for those wanting to acquaint themselves with critical, historical facts. The first hand, vivid accounts of the Italian families who suffered through this war will leave you feeling as if you were actually there with them on the farm."

—Don B. Cross, MBA, PMP
  Adjunct Professor, Brenau University
  4th Year DPA Scholar, Valdosta State University

"It has been a pleasure to read *Feeding the Enemy.* It has a personal touch throughout and provides insights to many sensitivities not always found in such a subject. All persons with interest in the subject either past or present should find it an easy and thoughtful treatment. I heartily recommend it as a most useful reference."

—David Harlow
  RADM, USN (ret)

"Fabulous read, I was unable to put the book down. If you love stories from the heart, this is the book to read."

—Gary Matheny, author of *If the Shoe Fits, Wear it. Life and Times of a Shoe Salesman* and *The Bullet*

Feeding the Enemy
by J.R. Sharp

Published by

◤ köehlerbooks™

210 60th Street
Virginia Beach, VA 23451
212-574-7939
www.koehlerbooks.com

Feeding the Enemy

J.R. Sharp

VIRGINIA BEACH
CAPE CHARLES

Dedication

This book is dedicated to my mother (Maria Cartelli) and aunt (Loretta Cartelli). If they hadn't shared their stories of survival, this book would not have been possible.

Table of Contents

Prologue

AS A CHILD LIVING in Italy, I remember sitting with my mother, aunts, uncles, and grandparents fascinated by the story of their survival. Their stories about World War II were remarkable. The majority of the stories surrounded what happened on the farm located on the outskirts of Cimpello. Cimpello is a small town located near the city of Pordenone in the northeast section of Italy about an hour from Venice.

The older I grew, the more vivid the stories started to become, and I understood why they talk so often about this period. The stories would become even more passionate when they would take out old photos and newspaper articles. Not all of the family and their friends survived, which would bring a lot of emotions into their storytelling.

I wrote this book based on their accounts of what happened during War World II. Most of the information in this book is based on at least two corroborating accounts and other research. Some accounts and dialogue are to some degree fictionalized due to the lack of information. All of the family names are true, but all other names and characters are fictional because of the lack of information during the writing of this book. All the events that occurred on the farm are non-fictional.

Chapter 1

Wounded

It was 1939 and the world was on the verge of war. Europe was already being conquered by the Germans, and in the Far East, Japan was making plans to be a world leader and had already invaded eastern China. America was on the sidelines after declaring neutrality and watching to see how things would unfold. Italy was also involved with its own world domination and was busy in Africa and the country of Ethiopia. The Axis Powers was formed, an alliance between Germany, Italy, and Japan during World War II.

Just as Adolf Hitler was leading Germany, a controlling Fascist leader named Benito Mussolini was leading Italy. "II Duce" had adopted Adolf Hitler's plans to expand German territories by acquiring all territories it considered German. The aim of invading Ethiopia was to boost Italian national prestige, which was wounded by Ethiopia's defeat of Italian forces at the Battle of Adowa in the 19th century, which saved Ethiopia from Italian colonization. Another justification for the attack was an incident during December 1934 between Italian and Ethiopian troops at Wal-Wal Oasis, where two hundred Italian soldiers lost their lives. In addition, Mussolini saw it as an opportunity to provide land for unemployed Italians and also acquire more mineral resources to fight off the Great Depression.

The war resulted in the military occupation of Ethiopia and its annexation into the newly created colony of Italian East Africa. After Italy joined the Axis, they attacked the British and Commonwealth Nations in June 1940 and pushed their way through Somaliland. It was during this period that most of the Italian wounded were shipped back to Italy. Among them was Gino Cartelli, an infantry soldier with 19 Infantry Division Venezia.

During the early stages of World War II, Germany's armed forces journeyed many times through the Italian countryside without any type of incidents with the locals. The German army worked very closely with the Italian Fascist and even had interpreters with them during most of their journeys.

In the later stages of the war, this all changed, and the German and Fascist-lead Italian forces became desperate for supplies and supporters. They started to collect metals at first but then confiscated food and other supplies from the local farmers and business owners. This was the same type of tactic used by the Germans on the Jews in Germany. In the northeast corner of Italy, it was especially difficult for the locals to hide their goods and family members due to their borders being surrounded by water and the country of Yugoslavia, which joined the Axis powers.

Local farmers were especially hit hard from most of these encounters with the military. They had to find inventive ways to hide their food and valuables. The Zucchet farm was such an example of how Italian farmers survived the war to end all wars.

***

Gino Cartelli was part of the military occupation after the Italians defeated the Ethiopian's in the Second Italo-Ethiopian War. He was part of the expansion of services division to run electrical power to the outposts in Ethiopia. The work was hard and extremely dangerous. Not only did they have to deal with the local natives trying to kill them and sabotage their work, but also the landscape was very rough and dusty. The diseases that the troops were exposed to were a variety of illnesses that included tuberculosis, malaria, and other respiratory infections.

With limited medical supplies and very few medical doctors, the army faced a dismal future. The animals and insects in this country were also strange to the Italian troops with most never seeing elephants, giraffes, hyenas, or lions until their arrival in this distant land. Gino himself had been awakened numerous times by hyenas coming to his tent to see if there was anything to eat. Most of the troops were from Italy, so most had never left their small towns and villages, and now they were being pushed into this type of environment, which was also very mentally hard to adapt to, this strange part of the world some two thousand miles away from home.

During an autumn morning in 1939, Gino's unit was running electrical power when his infantry unit came under fire from local units. Gino was just leaving the shower area when they came under fire. He raced to his tent to take cover and get his rifle when he was suddenly inflicted with some type of pain that he felt in his chest area. The wound didn't stop this young fighter, and he continued to his tent to take cover. After a short period, the shots stopped and Gino was able to see what the pain was all about and noticed blood. A bullet had punctured his chest causing enough damage that he fell to his knees and eventually passed out from the pain.

This minor skirmish with the locals would only wound Gino, but it started his journey back to Italy and to his lovely future bride, Catherina Zucchet. His company continued to provide electrical power to their outposts, not knowing what the future held for the Western Italian Empire.

Like other wounded or disease-stricken Italian troops stationed in Ethiopia, Gino's journey back to the coastline was not pleasant. Animals or large trucks traveling through rough terrain with little or no protection from the elements transported the majority of soldiers. Most of the wounded died. Gino finally arrived in an Ethiopian port in late 1939, and he was loaded on the transport ship headed to Treviso, Italy. Gino survived the return journey, but his future looked bleak because he had lost one of his lungs during the journey and was sick with malaria.

When he arrived in Treviso, the weak Gino Cartelli could barely move. The removal of his lung was also causing the young man complications. The long shipboard voyage from Africa through the Suez Canal and finally the coast of Italy had taken its toll on this young and brave infantry soldier. He drifted in and out of consciousness about the love he had left behind.

The farm that Catherina lived on was located about twenty kilometers from his hometown of Pordenone, which he had visited often before he joined the army. Catherina's parents were not pleased with her decision to be part of Gino's life, and he knew how they felt about him. He was going back to his love and wanted to prove to her parents that he could make her happy.

The hospital was understaffed and over its capacity with so many patients coming back from the Second Italo-Ethiopian War. All the patients were required to have family members present to take care of their war wounded, and Gino was fresh out of family members to help him recover from his injuries and disease-ridden body. During his first night in the hospital, he was in and out of consciousness and could barely make out the individuals attending to his needs. He woke up in the morning to see a priest on the left of his bed reading his last rights and a doctor on his right reading his chart. It was like a dream but better because for the first time in a long time he felt at peace and wasn't in fear of dying anymore. He could hear the doctor ask the priest if there were any family members to take care of this infantryman. The priest replied, "Just a young lady waiting outside in the hallway." Gino thought they were talking about the other individual next to him. The only young lady he knew was at the Zucchet farm some fifty kilometers away.

Catherina was sitting in the hallway waiting for the doctor and priest to finish with Gino. When they came out of the ward, she rose with shaky legs and felt nauseous. They walked past her and continued their rounds with no new news to give her about her loved one.

It was only two weeks earlier that she was sitting in the kitchen of the Zucchet farm main house that she was born and raised in talking politics with her father and mother. It was a Friday, her day to go to town for farm supplies, be with friends, and read the latest news about the occupation in Africa. Her father was very critical about all the expansion by the Fascist-led Italian government. The news about Germany upset him, too. In this part of the world, news was posted on the city town wall for all to read. This was also the place to read about the soldiers who had died or were wounded in action.

During a clear fall morning, Catherina went into the barn to get her bicycle to ride to town. Her parents always reminded her that she needed to look presentable before going to town and that she always wear a scarf covering her hair. Once she knew her mother and father could not see her anymore, she removed the scarf to allow her hair to flow with the wind. The roads were either made of dirt or cobblestoned and filled with an occasional traveler. As she was riding her bike through the farmlands and getting closer to the town of Cimpello, she could see the Pro-Fascist German interpreters standing and talking with their Nazi counterparts. With cigarettes dangling from their mouths and hats pushed to the sides of their heads, they stopped what they were doing to look at the lone Italian bike rider. The interpreters, Marco and Francisco, were from the local area and knew this beautiful young lady. Francisco yelled at her as she passed, "There is news of Gino!"

Francisco was a local farmer's son that her father wanted her to be with but she only had eyes for Gino. She stopped pedaling for a minute and coasted because her stomach had dropped to her knees. As she approached the meeting and dance hall that she and Gino shared those intimate times with each other so long ago, her legs started to give out on her, and she could feel herself getting lightheaded. She remembered how he could dance the night away and never got tired of moving his feet. Gino was six feet tall and one of the most handsome men she had ever seen. Many women said he looked like Errol Flynn the Australian-American actor.

As she continued down the main road of Cimpello, she passed the local restaurant, bakery, and meat market. As she got closer to the square, she could see the crowd of local villagers reading the news on the walls of the town hall. She noticed two of her childhood friends, Maria and Loretta; both were standing to the right of the crowd whispering in each other's ears. Catherina approached the center and immediately dropped her bike and ran through the crowd to read the news about her only love, Gino. Maria and Loretta rushed to her side to comfort her while she read the news; Gino was listed as wounded and in route to Treviso Hospital to recover from his wounds. The only way to get there was by train. The Italian government always requested family members to send help for the wounded because of the shortage of care providers at the hospitals. Maria asked Catherina, "What are you going to do? You know Gino's family won't send anybody to help him."

Gino was youngest of three brothers, and his father and mother did not travel. His father told him that if he left the family for a life in the military he was on his own. The father told his other sons the same thing as all three were fighting with the Royal Italian Army. Gino's father would not leave his home because of his business and his drinking issues.

Catherina looked at her two friends that she had known since birth and told them she wasn't sure what to do. Loretta said, "Catherina you must be with him. He is your one and only, and he needs your help." Catherina knew that she wanted to be with him, and it had been ten months since he left for Africa. But who would be helping on the farm if she left? Her father and mother were getting older and she had three brothers that where not much help. Her older brother, Chester, was fighting with Gino in Ethiopia. The middle brother, Bruno, was always sick and worked as a laborer for the railroad. Velasco was too young for farm chores. There was also Catherina's grandmother who lived upstairs in the small one-bedroom, second-floor room, and she was bedridden from polio.

Catherina's parents disliked Gino because he came from the wrong type of family. Her parents wanted her to marry another farm boy, Francisco the interpreter, but she wanted to be with the man that took her breath away, the man who always looked into her eyes like she was the only one in his universe. Gino had told her that when he finished his tour in the army they would be together for the rest of their lives. She needed to wait for him until he came back. Now he was back, but what type of wounds had he suffered? Catherina was full of mixed feelings as she grabbed her bike for the journey back home, forgetting the supplies and other tasks.

As she rode out of town, she could see Francisco talking with some of the young ladies that had questionable occupations. It looked like they were in some type of negotiation for favors, stockings, or cigarettes. Francisco saw her coming and blocked her path. She was afraid of riding around him and stopped her bike. She put her fingers through her hair and smiled at him.

"Thank you for telling me about Gino."

Francisco asked Catherina, "That is awful about Gino, are you going to do anything to help?" Catherina didn't want to be rude because she knew he had a lot of power and was known to use it. He also could place hardship on her family.

Catherina looked at Francisco and smiled and said, "No, not really. Why should I care about a fool and his dreams?" Francisco could only smile and place his hand on the handlebars of her bike and then a hand around her waist. She didn't move but quickly said, "Are you going to the rally tomorrow night?"

"Of course I am. My uncle will be back in town to speak to everyone, and I will be on the stage to support him, will you be there?"

"I will ask my father and mother if I can go, but they will only let me go if my brother Bruno is well enough to escort me. I must be going now; I must bathe my grandmother and help with dinner."

Francisco's smile vanished quickly with the thought of Catherina's grandmother. He stepped back, which gave Catherina time to start pedaling her bike back to the farm. Francisco yelled out to Catherina, "See you on Saturday with Bruno!" Catherina turned around on her bike and flashed him an inviting smile that quickly vanished when she turned around. She continued riding her bike down the dirt roads back to the Zucchet farm.

As she made the left off the main road and onto the stone driveway of the farm, she quickly dismounted. She could see Bruno sitting in front of the main house smoking a cigarette and said to him, "I have news of Gino." She ran with the bike to the barn and as quickly rushed back to the main house to talk with Bruno.

"Was there any news about Chester?" Bruno asked.

"No, but Gino was wounded and he is heading to Treviso to recover from his wounds and the government needs help at the hospital."

"What are you going to do?" Bruno asked.

She explained that she wanted to go to Treviso and help with

Gino, but that she needed his help to get her parents support and money. Bruno looked at her and knew this was going to be a tough sell.

"We need to team up on this and see if we can get them to send you and not for you to ask them for their permission."

Catherina thought this was a brilliant idea and kissed her older brother. Bruno got up from his chair very slowly and walked into the farmhouse with Catherina following him closely. Catherina noticed that he was getting weaker.

As they walked into the main kitchen their parents were sitting at the kitchen table talking about the upcoming winter and what was left to do before the cold set in. Pietro and Anna Zucchet always smiled at the first sight of their children no matter what was happening.

"Where are the supplies we needed, and what news do you bring?" Pietro asked.

Bruno, without missing a beat said, "Dad, most of the shops close early on Fridays when there is a rally on Saturday, Catherina just missed them before they closed."

Pietro looked at his children. "We need to remember that next week. You can go tomorrow early in the morning to get our supplies. Any news today?"

Bruno again spoke up as the elder. "I really miss Chester around the house; he was always making everyone laugh and was always the strong one. Do you miss him, Mom?"

"Yes, oh my God, is there bad news about Chester, please tell me?" Anna asked.

Bruno responded, "No, there is no news about Chester, but there are other families not so lucky. We should always try and help those others not as fortunate as us, since we have so much compared to the other families here in Cimpello."

"Son, I am very proud of you. Spoken like a true Zucchet."

"Dad, I really miss Chester and Gino being here to go to the rallies with me. They would always bring excitement to the cause, and we always would meet afterwards for drinks and dancing."

"It seems just like yesterday that they both left for Ethiopia with the crazy idea of expansion of this country," Pietro said. "Hell, we can't even feed our own people and we are out there conquering other countries like this is the Roman Empire again."

Bruno went on to explain that he saw Gino's father the other day and that he looked good, but that he missed all of his sons and that he was having a tough time getting by without any help and that his farm and brokering business was suffering.

"Well I wish there was something we could do to help out the Cartelli family, but we are strapped ourselves and barely making a living as well," Pietro said.

Bruno immediately captured the moment. "Dad, Gino was on the list of wounded soldiers and is on his way to Treviso to recover from his wounds."

"Well that is unfortunate," Pietro said. "But that is a good hospital. I spent a month there recovering from my stomach problems, remember that, Anna?"

Bruno explained that the government needed family members to help with the wounded but that the Cartelli's had no one.

"No, Bruno, you are too weak and sick," Pietro said. "Besides, you can't be in a hospital because you will get everyone sick from God only knows what you have."

"What about Catherina?" Bruno said. "She can go to take care of Gino?"

Anna took a step back from the table, waiting for the eruption from her husband. Pietro stood from the table, looked at his daughter, and preceded to the kitchen window, which overlooked the fields he had spent most of his life laboring over.

"Catherina, do you want to go help Gino?"

Catherina looked at her brother who was shaking his head up and down and said, "Yes, Father, I want to go because the Cartelli family needs our help. If the shoe was on the other foot, Gino would be helping our family."

Pietro looked away from the window and stared at his wife. "Catherina, you can go and help with Gino, but Bruno you will escort her to Treviso. As soon as he is better, you will return and go back to your chores. This trip will do you wonders and help you realize how good you have it here in this house and farm."

Pietro walked out of the house and Anna looked at her two children. "Well done you two."

***

The next morning Bruno and Catherina were in the kitchen having breakfast. Catherina went towards her mother as she was cooking and kissed her. "Thank you."

Her mother just smiled back and put her right hand on her daughter's cheek and said, "Be careful."

Earlier that morning Catherina was closing her suitcase when she saw a folded piece of paper on top of her clothes. It was an address in Treviso that her mother wrote down and some extra money. The address was a cousin of her mother. Catherina would stay at the cousin's house, which only had room for one. So Bruno would have to find his own lodging while in Treviso.

After breakfast Bruno and Catherina started their hour-long walk to the train station. Bruno was having problems keeping up with Catherina, but he just smiled at her knowing she was so excited about seeing Gino. He told her to go ahead and he would catch up, but she slowed down and waited for her brother.

There was a lot of commotion at the station. Pro-Fascist supporters were waiting for someone to arrive. Then it came to Catherina; they were waiting for Francisco's uncle. Bruno didn't want Francisco to see Catherina, so he told her to hide in the bathroom until the crowd was gone. As Bruno stepped up to purchase the tickets, he saw Francisco dressed in his uniform talking with one of the other supporters and immediately looked away for the fear of being seen. As he approached the counter, he heard Francisco call his name and wave for him to come over to him. Bruno bought two tickets for Treviso and put them in his pocket; he could hear the train coming and slowly walked towards Francisco.

"Bruno, are you going to Treviso to see Gino?" Bruno explained that he was going there to check up on Gino.

"So now the sick guy is a care taker and home maker," Francisco said smugly. "Tell Gino I said hi, but who is going to escort Catherina to the rally tonight, Velasco?" Bruno smiled at Francisco and explained that Catherina would not be making the rally tonight because she had other duties to attend to and that she didn't have an escort.

"Well I could escort her."

Just then Francisco heard his name called and both he and

Bruno could see his uncle coming towards them. Bruno saw his opportunity to leave and get Catherina.

The conductor was ringing the bell for passengers to board the train for departure to Treviso. Bruno saw Catherina and waved at her to get on the train in front of him. As she approached him, Bruno told her to keep her head down.

As the train rolled forward, Bruno could see Francisco staring at Bruno through the train window straight in the eyes with a disappointing look. Bruno felt relieved as the train rolled, fairly certain Francisco had not spotted Catherina. That relief quickly vanished when he saw Betty, one of Francisco's girlfriends. She was the one Catherina had seen Francisco with when she had rode her bike into town the previous day.

Betty was on her way to Treviso with the full intent to spend the money that she had earned just recently supporting the Pro-Fascist and Nazi campaign. Betty needed the latest fashions to ensure she always looked the part of the socialite.

The trip was only about two hours by train. Bruno explained to Catherina that once they determined Gino's condition he would return to Cimpello and make sure everything was good on the farm.

As the train arrived at Treviso, Bruno and Catherina noticed Betty getting off the train. He knew who she was and what she did and whom she would be talking with when she got back to Cimpello. She looked stunning with her blonde hair and light-blue dress with matching shoes and long legs. Bruno had gone to school with her and always thought she was good looking and dressed really nice. He told Catherina to go inside the main building and get directions to the house and that he would meet her outside the train station in about ten minutes. She gave him a puzzled looked and complied.

As she entered the building, she quickly turned to look out the window to see what her brother was up too. Bruno walked up to Betty from behind, took his hat off, and said, "You know you always look so pretty whenever I see you. How do you do it?"

"What are you doing here, Bruno?" she said.

Bruno put his hat back on and smiled. "I am here on family business and need to see some relatives about next year's harvest and visit a sick friend. What brings you here?"

"Well, I need to update my dress collections and Cimpello shops are just so out of date. Where are you staying while you're here?"

"I don't know yet, do you have any suggestions?"

"I always stay at the Continental. It is close to shopping and the train station."

"Well you shouldn't go strolling the streets by yourself in this big city. What time should I come back to escort you around today?"

Betty always wanted to be with good-looking men and needed reassurance that she was still the prettiest girl in the region.

"Meet me in front of the Continental in about two hours; I should be ready to go by then."

Bruno tipped his hat. "It's a date, see you soon."

"Who was that?" Catherina asked when her brother returned. "Isn't she Francisco's friend?"

"Don't worry about it, let's go find Gino."

They walked along the main road of the city and turned down the side street towards the house address from the note that Anna had written to Catherina. They found the house just as they entered the side street. Bruno knocked on the door. After a minute or two a slightly heavyset woman answered. She was dressed in a traditional light-black dress with matching shoes, her hair was pulled up in a bun, and she was wearing a white apron. She instantly grabbed Bruno and Catherina and started to hug them. It was their mother's cousin Patricia. She had not seen Bruno and Catherina in years.

"Oh my god, you both look great and all grown up. How was your trip?"

Patricia guided them into the town house and took a departing look around the street to see if there was anybody watching them. She lived in the town house with her husband and parents, but they didn't have any children. Patricia shut the door and escorted them both to the kitchen.

"How is your mother doing"?

Bruno said that she was doing just fine and that the farm and their father were healthy and so was everyone on the farm. As Patricia glided around the kitchen, Bruno and Catherina finally recognized her from family reunions at the farm. Patricia started a pot of coffee and asked Bruno if he knew of any places to stay at Treviso? Bruno replied that he had friends in the city and it wouldn't be a problem for him to find a place to stay.

"How do you both know Gino Cartelli?" Patricia asked.

Bruno said that Gino was best friends with their brother Chester and that his immediate family wasn't able to send anybody right away to take care of him. Catherina was looking out the window wide-eyed, nervously bouncing her knees.

"This is very nice of you to come and help your brother's best friend in his time of need," Patricia said. "Are you ready to see your room, Catherina?"

Catherina put her coffee down and made an up and down gesture with her head. Patricia grabbed Catherina's hand and led her down the hall and up a stairway to her room.

The room had a small bed and a nightstand with a small lamp. Catherina put her suitcase down next to the bed and started her way out of the room following Patricia down the stairs. When they returned to the kitchen, Bruno was outside smoking his after-coffee cigarette and looking at all the people walking by this side street on the main street. He thought to himself that there were a lot of people here and that he needed to escape rural Cimpello more often. The farm was no place for him, and he was getting older and needed to find something better for himself. He heard the door open and when he turned he could see Catherina coming down the stairs.

"Let's go to the hospital and see how Gino is doing."

***

They arrived at the hospital after about a five-minute walk. Bruno was having a hard time staying up with Catherina and smiled when he noticed how quickly his sister was walking. He called out to her to wait for him; she turned and looked at Bruno and for the first time noticed that he wasn't in the best shape and that his color in his face wasn't normal. She asked him if he was feeling sick.

"No, I feel fine. You just walk very fast and I am not a fast walker; I walk slower like dad. Catherina I am not going into the hospital. You know I haven't been feeling the best lately and don't want to make the sick any worse. You go in and come let me know how Gino is, and then we can decide what our next move will be to get him better."

Bruno waited by the main entrance. Catherina entered and noticed an information desk.

"Are you a member of the patient's family?" the information attendant asked.

"Yes, I am. I am Gino Cartelli's cousin from Cimpello, and I am here to take care of him. We saw that his name was on the wounded list in the square at home, and I am here at the request from the family to ensure his needs are met."

The attendant didn't even look at Catherina and started to check her list of patients.

"Private Gino Cartelli is on the second floor in the critical condition wing. You better hurry to see if you can do—"

Before the attendant could finish the sentence, Catherina went directly to the stairs leading to the second floor. As she entered the hallway, all she could see were doors on the left and right and an office in the middle. She hurried to the office where there was a lady asking for information about the location of her husband. Catherina got in line behind the lady and overheard the nurse tell the lady that she was sorry but her husband had passed away that morning from his wounds. Catherina would remember the widow's mournful bellow the rest of her life. Two nurses were helping the lady off the ground when one asked Catherina if she needed help.

"Would you like a glass of water? We are all so sorry about our soldiers that don't make it; they are all so brave and young. Are you here to see somebody?"

Catherina took a sip of water and finally looked at the helpful nurse. "Yes, I am here to take care of Gino Cartelli; he is my cousin."

"Let me look at my carts and see which ward he is in."

Catherina was shaking by now and felt like throwing up.

"Private Cartelli is in Ward 2A, bed 4 just down the hall to the left. Let me escort you so you can see him. We have chairs in the waiting room to the right, and after we see Private Cartelli, I will give you instructions on what will be required of you while he recovers from his wounds."

As they walked into the ward the nurse told Catherina about Gino's wounds and illness.

"He's very ill, so don't be shocked when you see him," the nurse cautioned.

In the room Catherina counted four soldiers when they entered. Each of the soldiers had a member of their family attending to their needs except for one next to the window. It was Gino. She waited for the nurse to leave and then rushed to his side and kissed his rough face.

Catherina looked at Gino for a minute and immediately noticed how awful he looked and noticed that he was unresponsive to her kiss. She kissed him again and left the room to find Bruno, who was leaning on the building smoking a cigarette and jingling coins in his pocket.

He was people watching, especially women in their skirts, high heels, and panty hose. He didn't have a care in the world. Catherina approached Bruno, and he immediately could see in her eyes that it wasn't looking good for Gino. She immediately ran into his arms for that strong hug that Bruno always gave her when things didn't quite work out for her.

"So how bad is Gino?" asked Bruno.

"He looks awful. The nurse said he had a lung removed in Ethiopia, and he also has malaria. I don't know how long it is going to take for him to recover from his wounds and the malaria, but you don't need to stay here in Treviso while I take care of him and spend all of your money on places to stay. You should go back to Cimpello and help father on the farm. They will need your help soon before winter sets in, and you know that he doesn't get around like he used to."

Bruno thought for a minute. "Well if that is what you want, and I am sure everything will be fine. You will need to write home every day and let mom know how he is doing. I will catch the morning train back, and if you need me to come back call the general store in Cimpello and leave a message for me, and I will return that day. You should go back in the hospital and see if Gino needs anything."

Catherina gave Bruno a big hug and kissed him then said goodbye to him and went back into the hospital to take care of her love. Bruno looked at his watch and thought to himself that he had time for a quick coffee before his date with Betty at the Continental.

***

Betty was looking at herself in the mirror that was hanging on the bathroom door, and she could tell that this was one of her better hair days and was ready to shop with her escort, Bruno. Although she was very jealous of Bruno's beautiful sister, she always thought that she was better looking than Catherina, and besides, she came from the farming side of the Cimpello and not the town side. Everyone knew that if you lived in the town you were better off than the farm folks—and more sophisticated. Even so, she liked Bruno who was very pleasant and handsome.

As Betty entered the elevator to go downstairs to meet Bruno, she thought about meeting Francisco's uncle the next day, which was the other reason for her being in Treviso. The thought of escorting a man twice her age wasn't pleasant. But she wanted to stay in good standing with the Pro-Fascist party, which took care of all her needs while she was in Treviso. This was a very nice arrangement and one that she wanted to continue and needed to make it during these tough times in Italy. The promises that ll Duce had made were not taking shape, and she was making it in her own way, even though most folks didn't agree with some of her choices. She was paid well and always put something away for her mother and father. The dream of becoming a countess was very strong and one that she really believed could happen if the Pro-Fascist movement took hold and she married Francisco. The rumor was that Francisco's uncle was a direct decedent of the royal family of Italy and that he would soon become the count of the Prodenone providence, which would encompass most of the northeast of Italy.

Betty entered the lobby from the elevator side and everyone immediately stopped what they were doing to look at the beauty of this woman. Bruno was sitting on the lobby couch smoking a cigarette. He stood when he saw her.

"Are you ready to go shopping for your new clothes?"

She smiled and kissed him on his cheek. "Yes, I am. Let's get going before the stores sell out of all their good dresses."

After three hours of shopping and walking, Bruno was exhausted but enchanted after spending most of the day with the beautiful Betty. As they arrived back at the Hotel Continental, Bruno looked at his watch. If he wanted to he could make the evening train back to Cimpello, but he would have to leave now.

Betty was leading the way and went directly to the elevator and told the elevator operator to take her to her floor. Bruno followed. As they reached her floor, Betty thanked the operator and walked towards her room.

"What a glorious day of shopping. We bought some very nice clothes for me, don't you think, Bruno?" As she reached for her key, Bruno again looked at his watch and then at Betty who was entering the room. She reached for her hat and threw the hat on the sitting chair and opened the window. Bruno looked at her behind and noticed how perfectly round it was. She turned around and leaned against the windowsill and looked at Bruno.

"You can put all the packages down beside my hat, and then come over here and look at the view, it is amazing." Bruno complied, took his hat off, and looked out the window with Betty at his side.

"Where are you staying tonight?" she asked.

"Well I haven't looked at any hotels yet, and there isn't any room at my friend's house. What do you think I should do?"

She put her right hand on his face and took his left hand and placed it around her waist. "I would let you stay here for the night but I have Francisco's uncle to pick up in the morning and take him around town. It wouldn't look right if I had you spend the night here, but we have time now to spend with each other."

She leaned in for the kiss she had been waiting for all day. Bruno responded with one of his famous kisses that the girls in Cimpello talked about at the dance hall. Bruno was enjoying the kiss and at the same time worried about Francisco finding out he had been with Betty. He broke from the kiss and looked into Betty's eyes.

"My dearest Betty, I would so much like to enjoy the rest of the afternoon with you here but I must catch the train back home this afternoon. My business here is complete, and I must help my father on the farm starting tomorrow before the ground gets too hard."

Betty's smile turned into a frown, and she thought to herself that mentioning Francisco was a mistake.

"My sweet Bruno, always thinking of other people before himself, that is why everyone loves you. If you must go home I understand, but if the train should pass you up or not come, I will be here trying on some of my dresses and practicing my poses."

"Betty, thanks for the offer, and I will surely be coming back if the train ride doesn't work out. You look amazing in all of your new clothes, but I must go now." Bruno leaned in for a goodbye kiss and made sure it was better than the first kiss he gave her. Betty could barely stand when he let her go; she felt weak in the knees and could barely catch her breath. When Betty opened her eyes, Bruno was gone, but not her urge for him. *There will be another time to make this happen*, she thought.

***

When Bruno exited the elevator, he looked at his watch and noticed that he had enough time to go by cousin Patricia's house and tell her that he was leaving.

"Where is Catherina?" she asked.

"She is with Gino at the hospital. Patricia, please tell her that I am leaving this evening and going back to Cimpello on the next train."

"I will, and have a good trip back. Tell your mother I will write her a letter soon."

Bruno waved back and turned and made his way to the station as quickly as his legs would take him. As soon as he arrived he noticed the train pulling into the station. He quickly ran to the ticket office and got in line. Luckily, there were other passengers waiting for their tickets for this train going to Cimpello and other destinations on this route so the train conductor was holding the train until the ticket office sold the last ticket to Bruno.

As the train pulled away from the station, Bruno felt a sigh of relief from today's events and really wanted to get back to Cimpello and relax. This excursion took a lot out of him, and he noticed that his energy was low. He glanced out the window one more time and then fell asleep for a well-rested ride back to Cimpello and the farm life.

***

It had been a week since Bruno left Treviso and Gino's condition hadn't changed. Catherina was becoming discouraged. Twice a priest had visited to give Gino last rights, and Catherina just couldn't believe that her love was ready to leave this earth. There was so much love that she could give to him. She promised that if he came out of this ordeal that she would be there for him for the rest of his life.

As the priest and doctor went past, Catherina got up and went back into the room to check on Gino. It was getting close to lunchtime and she wanted to make sure everything was ready for his meal. As she approached his bed, she noticed that the sunlight coming through the window was brighter than normal, and that his skin seemed to be more normal than the pale white that she was accustomed to this past week. The sheets were not wet and his eyes were steady and not moving rapidly back and forth either. As she approached, Gino suddenly moved his head towards the sunlight. Catherina grabbed his right hand and squeezed it, and he returned the gesture. She almost fainted from relief.

Catherina had not moved from that side of the bed for hours. She heard people talking and jumped nervously when she noticed that the priest was at the end of the bed.

"Oh, Father, I am sorry I didn't see you there, and you startled me for a moment."

"I am sorry if I startled you, my child. How is he doing this afternoon?"

"He seems to be getting his color back, and for the first time his sheets are dry, Father."

"Well that is good news. Private Cartelli has been one of our more difficult cases and hopefully this is a turn for the better. How long have you two been married?" asked the priest.

Catherina didn't want to say anything, but she couldn't lie to a priest, not with her strict Catholic upbringing. She remarked that they were not married and that she and Gino were very much in love and that they planned on getting married soon after this ordeal was finished.

"Let us pray for the full recovery of this brave soldier and that his bride-to-be gets her wish and that all that the Lord has to give is given to this wonderful couple that is before me here."

Catherina bowed her head and prayed with the priest for a few moments.

"I have to finish my rounds and will return later to see how he is doing. I will tell the doctor that he is doing better and see if he can come by and check on him, my child."

Catherina thanked the priest and just then the nurse walked in with some food and asked Catherina to see if Gino would eat. He did, but only small bites and without opening his eyes.

After the meal, the doctor entered and picked up Gino's chart and read for a little while and walked next to Gino and looked at his face. He checked his pulse and looked into his eyes, and then using his stethoscope listened to his heart. The nurse was standing next to the doctor waiting for the next set of orders.

"Let's see if this guy is going to make it. Nurse, go ahead and disconnect the IV and stop all medications. It is about time to see if we have broken the fever and see if this soldier's body can recover on its own." The nurse smiled and did as she was ordered, and for the first time since Catherina came to the hospital over a week ago, Gino wasn't hooked up to any type of IV or medication drip.

After a few hours the nurse returned and said, "Let's give this guy of yours a sponge bath and let you get home tonight." Catherina was sitting beside Gino's bed reading the Bible and shook her head in agreement. As the nurse put the small tub of water down on the table next to Gino's bed Catherina had already started to grab Gino from the back to turn him on his right side. Catherina grabbed the sponge and rinsed it in the tub and started to clean his back. Gino's body moved towards the nurse for the first time, and all of a sudden Catherina heard a voice.

"Who is getting my back wet? Where am I, and who is holding me on my side?"

Catherina dropped the sponge on the bed, took one step back, and put both of her hands over her mouth. The nurse was smiling and moving Gino back to his lying position.

"Catherina, am I lying on something wet? Is my bed wet?"

As he looked at her, he noticed a stream of tears coming from both eyes and her hands were over her mouth, covering the biggest smile that he had ever seen on her face.

"Well, young man, I guess you better roll over towards me

and let your bride grab that sponge from your back so you can finish your sponge bath."

"I need to go to the bathroom. Which way is the bathroom?"

"It is down the hall, but are you sure you can walk to the bathroom?" asked the nurse.

"Just try and stop me," Gino said with a smile. Catherina still hadn't said a word or moved since she removed the sponge. The nurse made a gesture to Catherina to help Gino get up and help him walk to the bathroom. Catherina rushed to his side as he got up from the bed and stood for the first time in over a week. He was dizzy but steady, and he held on to Catherina as he made his way around the bed. Catherina put Gino's right arm around her shoulder and started to walk with him towards the bathroom, which was down the hall in this hospital. The nurse handed Gino a cane to help him with his balance, but he declined.

"I don't need a cane. I am fine and can make this walk to the bathroom with Catherina." Catherina smiled at the nurse and started walking with Gino. For the first time she really noticed how thin he had gotten. He was always on the slim side, but now she could feel his bones surrounding his rib cage and his legs were very skinny. She needed to get him to start eating more and get his weight back up so he could recover from his wounds, surgery, and malaria.

Chapter 2

Fascists Emerge

PIETRO WAS READING THE paper in the kitchen and thought of his eldest son, Chester, who was in Ethiopia fighting for the expansion of Italy. He also thought about Chester's best friend, Gino, lying in the hospital in Treviso being taken care of by his beautiful Catherina. His third thought was of his town of Cimpello and what it used to be like before all the changes. The open markets, stores to shop in, restaurants to eat at, social events, and the evening walks that everyone would show up for in the middle of town. Now the town seemed like it was more of a recruiting station and Fascist rally center. Gone were all the social events and many stores and the restaurants—with the exception of the coffee shops—and the country and the Fascist supporters of Mussolini controlled everything. At least he had his farm that they didn't control and he could provide for his family. *It would only be a matter of time before they controlled all the food in the country, including this farm and all of the other farms in this area*, he thought.

Bruno walked into the kitchen. "So, Dad, how is your day so far? Need any help today? I was thinking about going to the train station and seeing if they need any help this winter. We could always use the extra cash for the farm, and I am close to getting my motorcycle."

"Bruno, before you go to the train station I want you to go to the Martin, Manzon, and Pelliccia farms and talk with the fathers and tell them we are having a meeting here at the barn tomorrow night at seven o'clock to talk about winter crops. Tell them that they need to bring their wives as well and that we will be serving dessert and wine."

"Dad, you never have meetings about winter crops. There are no winter crops. What is this all about?"

"Just tell them what I told you and no more. I will explain at the meeting. You need to be there as well. Tell nobody else about the meeting." Bruno shook his head and told his dad that he would go to the other farmers and relay his message to them before he went to the train station to look for winter work.

Bruno left the kitchen and Pietro returned to looking at his empty fields and the pump that provided all the water his family needed. Pietro heard a noise of someone coming into the kitchen, and he thought it was either Valasco or his newest and last addition to his family, his sweet little Valarie. But it was Anna.

"Any news from Catherina about Gino?"

Anna looked at her husband and just shook her head from side to side.

"Do you want something to eat? I plan on going to town tomorrow and checking the mail, do you want me to call my cousin to see how things are going?"

"No, she is an adult now and has to start making decisions on her own. Besides, this trip will do her good and make her stronger as a woman and maybe someday as a mother. Where are Valasco and Valarie?"

"They are outside playing in the front yard," Anna said.

"Tomorrow we are having a meeting with the other farmers in the barn to discuss the winter crops," Pietro said. "We will need dessert and wine for all those who are coming. I sent Bruno to tell everyone to come, and he is going to the train station to look for work during the winter. I am still mad at him for not staying with his sister in Treviso, but in retrospect it was good for him to come back and help out around here. My body isn't as strong as it used to be, my love."

Anna smiled at her husband. She knew what the winter crop meeting was about. Things were changing very fast and the farmers needed to stay ahead of what was coming or face a dismal future and life of poverty. Anna walked over to Pietro and gave him a hug, kissed him on his cheek, and went to the pantry to see about the dessert and wine for tomorrow's winter crop meeting.

***

Bruno arrived at the train station about ten minutes before the office was closing. He told all the farmers about the meeting. The Pelliccia family always acted superior to everyone else in the area because their farm and barn were larger than the other farms and they had more animals. But they did respect the Zucchets because they produced more crops that were of better quality.

As he entered the office, he could feel the tension coming from the office employees. Bruno had worked at the train station the previous year, and it had a more pleasant atmosphere than this year. He stepped up to the front office window and asked if there were any openings for workers this winter. The employment lady wore a uniform just like Francisco's. Bruno knew this was another sign that the Fascists were taking control of everything in the country. The lady recognized Bruno.

"Mr. Zucchet, we are going to need people for winter work. Please fill out these forms for us."

"Madame, this is a lot of personal information about my family and where I live, but not too much about me. Are these the right forms?"

The lady looked at the forms that Bruno handed to her and she smiled back at him. "Young man, those are the right forms. Please fill them out completely to ensure we can contact you about when you can come to work."

Bruno took the forms and noticed that there were about four other young men that he recognized that were filling them out at the community table in the middle of the employment office. He walked over to the table and took a moment to think about how he would answer. The questions made him uncomfortable, but he decided that his family could always use the money for the farm and, perhaps, he could buy a motorcycle. He decided to leave out some personal information about the members of the family, stating that he simply didn't know the answer.

After about twenty minutes of filling out the forms, he turned them in.

"When will we start to work this year," he asked the woman at the window. "Last year it was about this time?"

She looked at the documents he filled out. "Come back next week and we will be posting out in the front bulletin board who was hired and where they will be working."

"Will the pay be the same as last year?"

The lady just smiled at Bruno and said that she didn't have that information for him and that they were closed now. As Bruno was leaving the employment office, he noticed some of the men who had just applied for work hanging out having cigarettes. He recognized Marko and Anthony from school.

"How is the farm life treating you, Bruno?" Marko asked.

Bruno lit his cigarette. "Great. We had a good year and are hoping to be planting in early spring. How is your father's butcher shop doing?"

"Well, not so good," Marko said. "We're giving meat away to the army and not getting paid on time. Credit doesn't pay the bills and the banks don't care that you are feeding the enemy or the army, they just want their money."

"Anthony, I thought you were going to go to Rome and go to college," asked Bruno.

"Well I went down to Rome and went to school for about two months and then dropped out. The girls and wine got me in trouble. I will try again next year."

Damn, I didn't see that coming. Anthony was always so reserved and his parents were always so strict, Bruno thought. *I guess that is what happens when both of your parents are teachers and they don't let you spread your wings out when you're young. You go hog wild when you get your chance.*

Just as Bruno was finishing his cigarette the wind started blowing and he could feel the winter. He placed his hands in his jacket and started to move his body up and down to stay warm.

"What was with all those questions on the applications?" Marko asked.

"That was nothing," Anthony said. "You should have seen all the paperwork I had to do when I was signing up for college in Rome. It took me two days to finish all the paperwork and now look at me; I am standing in this breezeway freezing my ass off with you guys."

All of the men started to laugh, and Bruno asked if Marko and Anthony wanted to go get some coffee. They all agreed to go with him to the coffee shop.

As they walked to La Perla Café they could hear commotion from the inside of the café. Bruno walked in first and stopped before Marko and Anthony could get all the way into the café. Francisco and some of his Fascist supporters were having a heated conversation with the owner of the café. Bruno noticed their uniforms right away. This wasn't a good time to get coffee, but the owner saw three potential customers and waved them into his café.

Francisco approached Bruno, who stood at the coffee bar with his two friends. Bruno could smell the starch on Francisco's uniform and his pungent cologne.

Francisco lit a cigarette and threw a match into an ashtray that was between him and Bruno. He took a deep draw.

"Bruno, my friend. What are you doing in town? Shouldn't you be on the farm working?"

"I was applying for winter work at the railroad station like I did last year, then I saw Marko and Anthony, now we are having espresso."

Marko and Anthony both looked at Francisco nodding their heads in approval.

"So, when are you guys going to join the Fascist Party?" asked Francisco. "Finding work might be easier if you did."

Marko looked towards the owner and he turned his head and gave him a look of disapproval.

"Why should we join your party?" Marko asked.

"Well, for one reason, we just took over all the public transportation in this part of the country, and now we are looking to control most of the businesses in all of the towns, like this one. Isn't that right, Charlie?"

Charlie didn't acknowledge Francisco and served the espressos to his three customers.

"What is the matter, Charlie, you don't have anything to say?"

"Oh, I have a lot to say, but not in front of my customers," he replied.

"Well if that is how you get people to join your party you can count me out. It sounds like you are trying to bully the business owners into joining your crappy party." Bruno noticed that Francisco's face was turning red in color and he started to approach Marko.

"Francisco, if you come any closer to me, you are going to find yourself on the floor and that pretty uniform is going to be dirty," replied Marko.

Anthony and Bruno started to laugh because they knew Marko wasn't lying and could, in fact, hurt Francisco. Marko was in excellent shape and had thick arms. Bruno was laughing and noticed the other two supporters at the other end of the bar started to come to Francisco's rescue. They both appeared to be carrying axe handles. As they got closer Bruno, Anthony, and Marko took a couple of steps away from that bar and waited for the confrontation to start. Marko grabbed a barstool. Francisco raised his arms.

"Gentlemen, there is no reason for us to get into this situation over politics." He turned and made a gesture to his supporters to stop their approach.

"I agree," said Charlie, who was holding a shotgun in his arms and pointing it at Francisco's supporters. Bruno noticed that Francisco's face turned white from fear and that his legs were shaking.

"Charlie, there is no need for that gun. We were just leaving your nice establishment and will talk to you later about what we were discussing before your customers showed up," Francisco said.

"Don't bother coming back; my answer will not change so don't waste your time."

As the Fascist members left the bar, the boys returned to their coffee and Charlie returned the shotgun back under the bar.

"It is only a matter of time before they control the whole country and we all have to wear those uniforms," Charlie said.

Bruno looked at Marko and Anthony and wondered what would have happened if they got into a confrontation with them again. *Things are not changing for the better as promised by Mussolini and the Fascist party*, thought Bruno. He knew now why his father was having his meeting and what it was all about.

***

Pietro walked into the main house of the farm after working in the barn. He wanted to make sure that the barn was as clean as it could be, but it was a barn with horses, three cows, one bull, a couple of goats, and lots of chickens. He had moved the hay around to ensure there was a meeting area in the middle of the barn. The cows and bull were moved to the outer edge of the barn and the goats were moved outside. Pietro hated the goats but they produced milk and made the occasional good meal, plus, they kept the grass short.

"Anna, are we ready for the meeting tonight?" Pietro asked.

"Yes we are, and I checked the mail today and nothing from Catherina or anybody else," replied Anna. Velasco walked into the main room and Pietro looked at his third son.

"You are getting so big. How old are you now?"

"I am seven dad and getting stronger every day."

"Your mother and I need you to watch Valerie tonight while we entertain the neighbors in the barn. You need to keep her in the house and busy while we entertain our guests, do you understand me?"

"Yes, Papa, no problem," replied Valasco.

Pietro thought to himself that both his elder sons were going to leave soon and Valasco would be next in line to help him attend the farm. It was the routine of the family to teach all the boys how to farm, but with the future of Italy so uncertain Pietro didn't know how much longer he could keep the farm going.

Pietro had saved all the money he could over the years, but with winter setting in and the uncertainty of the country he had to make changes, or they would not survive the future. He was going to need the support of other farmers. Could he convince them that there was a need to start hiding assets and crops? It was only a matter of time before Fascists started to take from the farmers like they did during World War I.

Pietro was in the infantry during World War I and he remembered coming home and his father sharing stories of what the Germans did to this farm and what he did to survive. Italy was not at war yet, but ever since Italy joined the Axis Powers, it was getting the cold shoulder from most of the other countries in Europe. Pietro knew this from reading the papers and having long discussions with the other farmers. This included the businessmen in Cimpello during the weekly auction house gatherings. Hitler was making his move to spread his power in Europe, and Italy was doing the same in Ethiopia.

"Anna, how much wine do we have? You know that the Pelliccia's love to drink wine and they don't stop drinking until it is time to go." He put his hands around his wife and started to look into her eyes, and she looked deeply back into his. They kissed each other quickly and just as fast let go of each other because there were children running around the house.

"There is enough wine for all to have and dessert as well. Did you clean up the barn?"

"Of course I did, my love, only the best for you," answered Pietro.

"You know you two should hug more often," said Bruno, who was standing in the kitchen entrance, unnoticed by his mother and father. Pietro looked at Bruno and told him to shut up and quit being so disrespectful to his parents. He smiled at his father and was finishing his apple when he told his father he needed to talk to him about what happened in town yesterday.

"Let's go outside and talk, I don't want to upset your mother."

Both men exited the main house through the door leading to the white cobblestone driveway. The main water pump with an attached washbasin provided all the fresh water the family needed. There was a bench that Pietro made decades ago that was located next to the house right underneath the main room window. The bench was still in great shape after so many winters and hot summers. It was here that Pietro and his sons had their long conversations about politics and any other topics that interested them. They sat down on the bench and Bruno lit a cigarette while his father smoked his pipe. Pietro listened to his son while smoking his pipe and moving his left hand up and down his suspenders.

"Bruno, we need to limit our time in town, my son. Only go there for business and leave. No more socializing or loitering in Cimpello or you will find yourself being taken away without anybody knowing what happened to you. Francisco and his family are in deep with the party and we need to stay clear of them and any other member of the Fascist Party. They will come after this family and the farm. If they have taken over the train station and all of the public transportation, it is just amount of time before the businesses are taken over. Just like they did in War World I, and most of the businesses did not fair very well and eventually closed their doors. Then there were lines for food and services that never came."

Pietro paused and looked at his son. "You probably need to watch yourself if you get that job at the train station. We could use the money but I would rather you be here at the farm."

Bruno nodded at his father, and they both looked out to the fields and the sun setting in the west. Anna, who was listening from the window, walked away from the main room window clutching her hands in her apron and trying not to cry. *What is happening to Cimpello and Italy?* she thought. *Why can't we just live to live and not try to kill each other?* She headed for the kitchen to finish getting all the food and wine ready for the evenings meeting.

* * *

Pietro was checking on his feed for the cows when he heard the first family arrive; it was Greg and Martina Martin. Of all the families that lived in this area, Greg and Martina were their best friends and could always be counted on for support and comfort. Next came John and Mary Manzon by bikes, and finally, the Anthony and Gilda Pelliccia family by truck, accompanied by Anthony's strong-willed mother, Loretta.

Pietro didn't dislike any of his neighbors, but he tended to like some better than others. He often wondered why the Pelliccia's always dressed so nice and looked like they were going to church; even Anthony looked nice working in his fields.

Anna greeted all the wives and ladies at the entrance of their barn and took whatever desserts that they brought and set them down next to hers in the center of the barn where the wine was being poured by Bruno. There were seats available for all, but most of the men preferred to stand and talk. They all shared stories about their families, kids, grandkids, and the newest farming innovations while they sipped wine and ate Anna's *torta margherita*, the perfect Italian pound cake for the cold weather, and other desserts brought to the Zucchet Farm. After about a half hour Anthony Pelliccia finally spoke up.

"Pietro, now that we are all here what is on your mind?"

Pietro got up from his chair and stepped towards his wife and took a sip of his wine and put his right arm around her waist for support. Bruno stopped what he was doing at the wine table and walked towards his father to show his support. Pietro finally spoke.

"Some of you remember what happened to this area during the last war and how hard this area was hit from loitering from the army and other groups. We lost a lot of farmers during that period and only a few of us survived those very tough times. Well, my friends, I remember too vividly coming back from the war and seeing the devastation and how hard it was for my family to get our farm back to where it is today. I don't want the same thing happening again and feel that if we band together as one we all will survive what is ahead of us. If we go our separate ways it will be harder for us to survive."

After Pietro spoke, there was silence in the room for at least a couple of minutes. All you could hear were the animals moving, the wind outside, and the occasional movement outside of birds, owls, or bats. Anthony was the first to speak.

"Pietro, the last time I checked, we were not at war and this year's crop was the best it has been in years, and all of our farms made excellent profits from the auction house."

"I have to agree with Anthony," remarked John.

Pietro looked at Greg and waited for him to speak up. Greg didn't say anything and just looked at Pietro with his deep green eyes and knew what Pietro was going to say next and would support his longtime friend in this endeavor. Pietro put his glass down and started his speech that he had practiced all day.

"Anthony, you are absolutely correct, but for how long will this country not be at war? Some of us have sons and friends of our families overseas right now doing nothing but trying to expand our countries territory; this is not the Roman Empire anymore. Why is this country in Ethiopia and Albania? What about the Germans and Hitler? They have already invaded Poland and will not stop there. This is the same thing they did over thirty years

38   FEEDING THE ENEMY

ago, and what happened then? It is just a matter of time before they come for our crops, cattle, and whatever else they need so they can keep on conquering. We have already seen the Germans on the streets, and what about the Pro-Fascist movement here? They have already taken the public transportation system and have started taking the businesses away from their owners in the name of Mussolini. Who will be paying us next year? We need to stay one step ahead of them or we will never be able to survive what the future is of this territory or country."

For the second time that evening there was silence in the barn. This time it was a very sober one and it was felt by each of the families. They all knew this was coming but didn't want to believe this was going to happen again. Then Loretta spoke up.

"You're being ridiculous, Pietro. We have assurance that this will not happen to us by the Fascist Party. Without the farmers this country will fold and nobody will survive the year without food."

Anthony looked at his mother and wife and back at Pietro. "I have to agree with my mother, Pietro; this will not be happening again. We had the Party at our house just the other week and they assured us that we would be taken care of during this transition of our country."

Pietro looked at Anthony and thought, *How can this guy be the best farmer in the territory and be so gullible?*

"Bruno, please share your story of what happened at the café yesterday with our friends," Pietro said.

After Bruno finished his story, all the families looked at each other with disbelief.

"Are you sure they had axe handles and were trying to shake him down?" Anthony asked Bruno.

"Yes, this was not a simple argument, and I know what I saw and heard."

"When was the last time any of us has been in town for the evening walks?" Pietro said.

There was a long pause and everyone just looked at the ground for answers. "That is my point. We are all hoping this goes away and everything goes back to the way it was, but it hasn't and it is getting worse. We need to start now or we will be sorry."

Finally Greg spoke up. "What do you want us to do, Pietro?"

Without missing a beat, Pietro responded, "We need to start storing more feed, hay, food, metal, wood, and anything else that we will need in the future. All the farms have strengths and weaknesses, if we ban together and built on each other's strengths then all of us will survive this uncertain future. Here is a good example, for some reason Greg's crops mature before any one of us, and my crops always are the last to come to production. Let's all share equally with each other and we all will help who doesn't have that great a crop or who is getting loitered more than the rest of us. All of us need to grow something different every year like corn, lettuce, cabbage, carrots, potatoes, or something that we can all use. Then the next year we change the fields again, so we always stay ahead of what group is loitering from us and store for the winter. Each of you need to find places in your farms to hide food, metal, wood, and whatever you are going to need, and you must keep these places secret from all those who will do you harm."

Pietro was done speaking and felt exhausted after he was done and hoped everyone was on board. He was sure that if they did not band together they would all probably be doomed. Without even waiting for anybody to answer, Greg spoke up.

"Count the Martin's in."

"The Manzon's are in as well," John said.

They all turned and looked at the Pelliccia family. Anthony looked at his wife and then his mother and said, "I don't agree with what was said in here and believe that all of you are overreacting to this situation that happened in town." Anthony's mother smiled because she knew her son was the smartest in the bunch. Anthony's wife, Gilda, was good friends with Anna and looked at her with fear in her eyes because she knew in her heart that Pietro was right.

"Well, Anthony," said Pietro, "I am sorry you feel that way—"

Anthony interrupted. "I am not done yet, Pietro, let me finish speaking before you take my wine away and send us home. Like I said, I believe everyone in here is overreacting to this situation, but my father, God rest his soul, did tell me often about the hard times that fell on this area back in the last war. We too took a long time to get back to profit and now are doing very well. I want to continue this and will join you in this endeavor of yours, Pietro. I would rather be prepared than be loitered into poverty."

Anthony raised his glass. "So here is to Pietro's plan and the future of all of our farms!"

Chapter 3

Hiding Places

CATHERINA SAT BESIDE GINO'S bed while he slept, and as she looked up from the daily newspaper she could see that he was getting stronger and had started to gain some weight. He was so skinny when she arrived here weeks ago, but now it was just a matter of time before he would have to go back to the army. She wondered what would happen to him and if they had any future together after she returned to Cimpello.

Gino had been in this hospital for over a month and nobody from his family came to visit him. Catherina thought that was very sad and knew that if anything ever happened to her brother Chester there would be a line to help him out.

It seemed to be colder here in Treviso and Catherina was always covered up in layers of clothing that really didn't make her feel very pretty; or maybe it was the hospital that was cold. The building was very old and she couldn't walk past a window without feeling a draft. It was a wonder that most of the patients didn't have some type of cold or pneumonia from all the drafts, but they did have plenty of blankets available. Catherina used them to stay warm while watching her beloved Gino.

It was getting close to lunch when the nurse, Trisha, and Father Russo came by to see how Gino was doing.

"Well this one has come a long way since he first arrived. I know I gave him his last rights at least three times but it wasn't his time yet. Plus his beautiful Catherina being here has also helped, and she has been taking such great care of him. You know if you want to get married I can perform weddings here in the rooms. I have done many of them over the years."

The nurse was smiling from ear to ear and looked very guilty for conspiring with Father Russo. She put Gino's lunch down next to his bed and stood next to Father Russo. Catherina just smiled at both of them and remarked that she needed to wake up Gino for his lunch.

"I need to go finish serving lunch to the other patients, and Father Russo don't you need to see other patients?" remarked the nurse.

Gino stirred and looked at Catherina. "What was all that about?"

Catherina just shrugged her shoulders. "Father Russo was just saying how remarkable it was that you have come so far in your recovery, and the nurse was just bringing your lunch."

Catherina gave Gino his napkin so he didn't spill his meal on his hospital nightgown. Gino hated the gown and wanted to wear his own clothes, but he had none and needed some eventually. As Catherina adjusted the hospital bed, Gino was eating his bread and pouring himself some water. Catherina looked at the window.

"It's dark in here. How about we open these drapes for some light." Gino nodded approval. As Catherina moved the drapes to let some light into the room she noticed that it was a very nice day, even though it was winter and cold. She adjusted the blanket around the bottom of the window to stop the chill from coming into the room and heard Gino clear his throat and begin to speak.

"Catherina, you know I have always cared about you and never stopped thinking about you the whole time I was gone. You mean so much to me and since my family doesn't even care about me, I really do consider Chester and you as my family. I miss your brother and hope he is doing well in Ethiopia."

Catherina turned around and gave him a seductive look, brushing her hair over her shoulder.

"That was very nice to say, and I missed you as well, and you really do mean a lot to our family or my father wouldn't have let me come here and take care of you," she replied.

Gino smiled and thought, *This is the moment I have been waiting for.* Gino took a deep breath and looked deep into Catherina's eyes.

"Honey, why don't we take advantage of Father Russo here at the hospital, and then you will be taken care of for the rest of your life if something should happen to me. What I am trying to say is will you marry me, Catherina Zucchet?"

She almost fell to her knees and looked at him with her big eyes and started to cry. Catherina moved closer to the bed and put her left hand on the right side of his face and then continued to move her fingers through his hair. She moved her head closer to his and simply said, "Yes, Gino Cartelli, I will marry you!"

Before he could say or do anything she was kissing him more passionately than she had ever before, and he noticed that she was crying at the same time that she was kissing him and shaking as well. He returned her kiss and started to smile. At the same time he placed his right and left hands on both of her cheeks to make this kiss one that she would never forget. After about two minutes they both let go and started to smile and laugh.

Nurse Trisha, who attended to Gino most of the time, was at her station when Catherina walked up to her and told her the great news. She immediately gave Catherina a big hug and said, "I knew you guys were going to get married, you looked so right for one another. We must go find Father Russo and let him know that you two want to get married here at the hospital."

"What about rings?" asked Catherina.

"The church will provide you with rings, and the army will pay for them. They want their men married so they will fight better for their country."

Catherina returned to the room and told Gino that the nurse was going to find Father Russo and give him the news.

"I must tell Patricia that we are getting married. She has been so kind to me and let me stay at their house for this past month. She will be my maid of honor, if that is alright with you."

Gino just nodded approval. He still wasn't very strong and he needed at least another month to recover from his surgery and malaria.

"I will need to tell my mother and father at some point, but I don't want them to come out here for the wedding. What do you think we should do about them?"

"Well why don't we just get married and let them know later on so there is less for them to worry about if everything you say is true about what is going on in Cimpello."

The nurse entered the room with Father Russo and both of them looked very happy and pleased.

"Let's see if I understand the situation here; you two want to get married, and when do you want this to happen?"

"As soon as possible if that works for you, Father," Gino said.

"Well, my son, I have never given a soldier his last rights three times and then had that same soldier come back from the other side to ask me to perform a marriage. It is rare indeed, and the Lord works in mysterious ways, and I am only his humble servant. So what about tomorrow? Is that too soon?"

Gino looked at Catherine who nodded. "That will be fine, Father Russo. Tomorrow it is," said Gino.

***

Catherina walked down the main road of Treviso from the hospital and headed towards the house of her mother's cousin Patricia. Her mind was swirling with all that just occurred at the hospital and wondered if this was the right thing to do in her life. It was cold again and she always wanted to get married in the spring, but Catherina wanted this man and didn't want to wait. She really wasn't looking at getting married at the young age of twenty-two, but she really loved Gino, who was twenty-seven. He was smart, gentle, and very good-looking, and he was best friends with her brother Chester. She always thought that her father didn't like Gino, but why would he approve of her coming here to take care of him?

She needed to get a dress for the wedding ceremony and needed Patricia's help. As she turned right towards the house she could see her cousin sitting on her chair and looking out the window. The street was located in an ideal place and was blocked from most of the wind, so it always seemed that it was warmer in the house. As she headed towards the house, Patricia jumped up from her chair and looked at Catherina as if something was wrong.

"Why are you home so soon, is everything okay with Gino?"

Catherina just smiled. "Gino is doing just fine, but I need a dress Patricia, and I need your help to go buy one for tomorrow."

"Okay, let me get my coat and purse and we can go get you a dress. What kind of a dress do you need, and why do you need it by tomorrow?"

"I am getting married tomorrow and need a better dress than the ones I brought with me!"

Patricia took both of her hands over her mouth and yelled. "Oh my god, you are getting married. Hurry up and get into the house. We need to get so much done by tomorrow. Have you told your mother yet?"

Catherina opened the front door of the house and stepped into her open arms, and what a huge hug she gave her.

"We must tell your mother that you are getting married. We need to call Cimpello and leave a message for her to come tomorrow. What time is the wedding?"

"The wedding is at one o'clock, and would you be my maid of honor?"

There was only ten years difference in their ages and Catherina had become very close to Patricia in the past month and considered her like a big sister more than a distant cousin.

* * *

It was about eight o'clock when they finally got back home. The dress was picked and so were the shoes. The dress was getting tailored and would be ready in the late morning. It was white and off the shoulder with floral patterns in the lower section of the dress. The dress was mid-way to her ankles from her knees and, of course, she would be wearing silk hose for the first time in her life. Patricia bought the hose for her as a wedding gift and they were almost the same price as the dress. Catherina felt like a princess when she tried on the dress. It really wasn't a wedding dress in the traditional sense but it would work in this situation. Patricia would be going to the market first thing in the morning on the way to pick up the dress to see if they had flowers for Catherina. With winter setting in, it would be hard to find any type of flowers for this small wedding. If there were any flowers, they would be from Africa, but she knew it was a long shot.

As the ladies settled in for the evening and were in the kitchen having supper, Patricia asked Catherina a question that stopped her in her tracks. What was she going to do if Gino went back to Ethiopia?

Catherina looked down at the floor and then looked at Patricia. "I love Gino and will wait for him no matter where they send him, but he doesn't think he will be sent back overseas because of his wounds he suffered. He has to be medically qualified for service and he is still recovering from all his wounds and malaria."

Patricia smiled and finished handing Catherina the last of the dishes to wash, and as she leaned against the kitchen counter she could not help but ask her some other deep questions.

"If Gino gets to go home, where are you two going to live, and what will he do for work?"

Catherina was starting to get cold feet. Gino never really talked about any of these issues in the hospital.

"There is one thing I know about my Gino, he is very good at anything he does so getting a job in Cimpello will not be a problem. We can stay at his father's house or the Zucchet farm until we get a place of our own. There is plenty of room at both locations, and I have my own room on the farm that he can share with me."

Patricia nodded approval. "Well, young lady, tomorrow is your big day. You will need your sleep and it is getting late. I am going to bed, and I will see you in the morning."

Catherina gave her cousin a hug and thanked her for all of her help today, and both of them headed in the direction of their bedrooms. As Catherina entered her room, she started to cry but couldn't figure out why. Was she crying because she was scared, excited, or happy? All she knew was that she needed to stop because if not her eyes would be puffy in the morning. So she got ready for bed and turned out the one lamp in the room and soon she was asleep.

***

Gino was opening his eyes for the first time on this special day and he noticed an army uniform hanging next to his bed. He wondered whose uniform it was, since he had been wearing hospital gowns for as long as he could remember. Nurse Trisha walked into the room carrying his breakfast.

"Good, you're awake, now we can see if this uniform will fit you for your wedding today." She placed his meal on the table next to his bed and gestured him to get up and try on the uniform. They also had some new army issued underpants and T-shirts.

"Where did you get that uniform from?" asked Gino.

"We have our ways," the nurse said. "But you must get up and try it on since we only have so much time to get you ready for your wedding. It is always a wonderful event, the wedding, and in this place. It's something special that we don't get very often. We mostly only see the bad side of life and not the good, so you and Catherina are very special to us here at the hospital. There are going to be lots of hospital staff here to watch your ceremony, so get up and try on this uniform!"

Gino smiled at her and began to get out of bed when he noticed that he was the only one in the room. Both of the other patients had been moved and as Nurse Trisha was walking out of the room, Gino asked, "Hey, where are the other two patients?"

"We moved them to the other rooms so we could get all of your guests in the room to watch the ceremony. I will be back in ten minutes to see how the uniform looks."

Gino got to his feet, and he was dizzy again and wondered if it would ever stop. He could not leave the hospital until the dizziness stopped and he was able to walk down the hall and back on his own. That hallway was a long way, and he could hardly get to the door of the room. He struggled a little with the top of the uniform because it was a little tight, but the pants and everything else was fine. Gino felt a little weird without shoes but the nurse said that they didn't have any shoes. *Guess I'll be married in socks*, he thought.

Just as he was finishing getting dressed, the nurse returned and looked at Gino with a great big smile. "You look amazing, and how does the uniform fit?"

"It is a little tight, but other than that it feels great."

"Now we need to get you shaved and bathed before your bride gets here."

Nurse Trisha was looking at Gino and he could see her eyes

start to tear up. She was brushing the uniform with her hands when she looked at Gino.

"How you survived is amazing, and all the doctors still talk about you every day. You need to take the top off so you don't spill anything on it and finish your breakfast. I will be back in ten minutes to help you to the bathroom so you can get ready for your wedding."

Patricia and Catherina had arrived at the hospital around twelve-thirty. The dress fit like a glove and the shoes were perfect. Catherina was able to get her hair done with the local hairdresser on the way to the dress shop. Patricia was unable to find flowers and was disappointed, but that wasn't going to stop this wedding. As they made their way to Gino's floor, Catherina was getting very nervous and feeling a little sick to her stomach. She had to sit down in the dressing room, which was the women's bathroom, to catch her breath, and Patricia was able to get her a little breakfast from the nurses so she was able to feel better. Gino was already waiting for Catherina, and Patricia went to the room to see how everything was looking, and also to see how Gino was doing. She hadn't seen him in over a week and could tell right away he was looking much better as she entered the room. *He does look like Earl Flynn with that uniform on*, she thought. His hair was combed back and he had had a fresh shave.

"Are you ready to get married, Gino?" asked Patricia.

Gino was sitting in the only chair in the room and was feeling a bit nervous because there were more and more people coming into the room.

"Yes, I am. How is my bride doing this afternoon?"

"She is fine and getting dressed right now. She has a beautiful dress and shoes to match. You will be pleasantly surprised."

Father Russo entered and asked if anybody had seen the bride and if they were still ready to go at one o'clock.

"She is in the dressing room and will be ready in about ten minutes," Patricia said.

Father Russo approached Gino. "Are you ready to do this, young man, and can you stand up?"

"Yes, Father, I am ready, and I'll stand as long as the ceremony will last."

Father Russo looked down at Gino and put his right hand on his left shoulder. "Perfect, so now we will wait for your bride to come and get you two married."

It was exactly ten minutes later and Gino could see everyone turn to see Catherina coming towards the room. He knew that was his cue to get up, and he did so. As she entered the room, Gino was speechless and could only stare at his beautiful bride.

* * *

Bruno walked into the main house and was holding an envelope in his hand. He shouted for his mother and father who were in the kitchen having coffee. His mother was at the sink doing dishes and his father was at the table with Velasco and Valerie finishing breakfast.

"We have a new member of the family as of this afternoon," Bruno announced. Anna immediately turned around and started to wipe her hands with the dishtowel, but Pietro didn't even stop drinking his coffee.

"Well it's about time," he said. "I was wondering how long it would take. They always seem to be happy when they are together."

Anna grabbed the letter from Bruno and started to read it.

"Father, I thought you didn't like Gino," Bruno said.

"I don't like any guy trying to take my daughters away from the farm," Pietro said. "They are great helpers and do the chores we men don't like to do, isn't that right, Valerie?"

Valerie just looked at her father and went back to her doll. Anna just shook her head disapprovingly. Pietro laughed and winked at his wife.

"Pietro, they are getting married this afternoon. There is no way we could make the wedding," Anna said. "Why would they get married so suddenly, unless Gino wasn't doing well, but the letter says they are all doing fine?"

Pietro went next to his wife and put his right hand over her shoulder as she started to cry.

"Honey, who knows? We won't know the answer to those questions until she comes back from Treviso. Or call and leave Patricia a message. Maybe we can find out from her. I just want to know where they are going to live when he comes back from the army. We are getting tight here in this house. Bruno, we need to talk, and did you get the things from town that I asked you to get?"

"Yes, I got everything, and I did get a job with the railroad this winter, and we start next week," Bruno said.

Bruno had gone to Cimpello early in the morning to check on the status of his job, get messages, and buy a metal box and the largest container he could find. It was market day and a lot of venders came from out of town to sell their goods. Gypsies made their rounds as well. Bruno had a tough time with the container and was glad he took the cart that he pulled with his bike.

"Where did you get the container and box?" Pietro asked when Bruno returned.

"From the Gypsies, Dad, they always have this kind of stuff. You just don't ask where they get their stuff from," Bruno said with a grin.

Pietro started to laugh and told his son he did well and that they needed a good hiding place for the container and metal box. Bruno finally asked his father what he was going to hide in the container and box.

"Son, the future doesn't look good for this farm, and we need to get ready for what is ahead. We need to bury that container where nobody but your mother and I know where it is. We'll keep food in it. That way, when and if the loiters and soldiers come here to take our food, we at least have enough for ourselves. The metal box is to hide our money, jewelry, and metal objects. Hurry up and find a place for that container. I have some beans and corn to put in it and I don't want them to freeze." Pietro looked at his son and winked at him.

"Anna, you and I need to get all of our valuables together, including your wedding ring and necklaces, and put them into this box. Only wear cheap stuff that you will not miss. The Fascists will be coming soon. When you go to town tomorrow, go to the bank and do what I told you to do."

***

Anna woke up early and got the children ready and walked them to school as she always did during winter. Pietro and Bruno were still asleep after being up late burying the container. As she exited the house with her two youngest, she could not tell where the container was buried. *They did a great job*, she thought.

After Anna got the children to school, she went to town to send a message to Patricia, and then went to the bank as instructed by her husband. This was not the first time she had gone to the bank after dropping off her children, but it was the first time she requested coins instead of paper lira. Anna knew that the teller would ask her why she wanted the coins and she had the answer. She hated to lie, but she knew it could mean the difference between surviving the future or not and she would do anything for her family. After she sent her message to Patricia, she went to the bank and filled out the proper paperwork for her money. They wouldn't take all of their money but slowly withdraw what Pietro thought they would need in case of an emergency. Anna got in line, which was smaller than usual. She passed the withdraw slip to the teller, who started counting out paper lira. She was wearing a Fascist Party uniform.

"I'd like coins please," Anna said.

"Mrs. Zucchet, you never get coins; you always get paper lira. Why are you requesting coins?"

"Didn't you hear that Gino and Catherina got married? We want to give them a gift. In our family it is tradition to give coins instead of paper money because metal lasts longer than paper and we want their marriage to last as long as the coins."

The teller gave her the biggest smile and took back the paper money and started to count out the coins as requested by Anna. "That is very sweet and what a great tradition your family has. Please tell Gino and Catherina I wish them all the happiness. Where did they get married?"

"They were married in Treviso; it was a military wedding. We couldn't make it because of the children."

As Anna was leaving she noticed a gathering at the center of town. She decided to see what was going on. She saw Gino's father in the middle of what was going on and she wondered if he knew his son was married. Gino's father always seemed to be involved with just about anything going in Cimpello. The town's auctioneer was always involved with matters concerning cattle, crop, and beans, but Mr. Cartelli tended to be a little more than involved. Some would say that he was borderline nosey. It didn't help his reputation that he liked to drink and gamble his money away. There was a family farm, but he had not been taken care of it ever since he became the town's auctioneer. Anna noticed that there were quite a few Fascist supporters and for the first time she noticed Germans with them as well.

Gino's father was really mad and yelling at all the uniform personnel. As she got closer to the center of town, she noticed that the mountains were full of snow and the clouds were grey. It was getting colder as winter was in full swing. In the summer time it was harder to see the mountains due to the heat, but in the winter it was a daily occurrence. She wrapped her scarf around her face to protect her skin and also to protect her identity. What she noticed was that there were other town employees with Gino's father and they also were visibly upset, but most were just listening to Gino's father yelling.

It seems that they were being told that their jobs were no longer needed. Mr. Cartelli was telling them that they had no authority to cut their jobs and that they were all fools in uniforms. Anna noticed that there were a couple of Germans in a car watching. Just about the same time as Mr. Cartelli was making some insulting remarks, one of the German soldiers walked towards Mr. Cartelli, reaching for what looked like a pistol from his left side. He walked briskly to the right of Mr. Cartelli who did not see him and struck him in the back of his head with the butt of the revolver. The German officer then looked at one of the Fascist supporters, which was Francisco, and told him something in German. Francisco had a look of surprise and shock and told everyone to go to their homes and that there was nothing left to discuss.

As she rode down the long road to the farm, Anna noticed the German car driving past her on the parallel road, leaving town. There was a bigger truck behind the German car and it was full of troops. They all were looking at Anna as they drove by. As she pulled into the driveway, she got off the bike and started to walk the bike to the main house. Pietro and Bruno were outside having coffee. As she approached the main house, Pietro could tell that something was wrong.

"What is wrong, my dear? Did you have problems in town?" She explained what she saw. Pietro looked at her and got up from the bench and put down his coffee and gave her a big hug.

"You are so brave, my dear wife, and you will not go back into town again. Were you able to go to the bank and get what I asked you to withdraw?"

"Yes, I did get the money, but please don't ask me to go back to the bank again."

"Bruno, you are going to have to go to town from now on to get what we need," Pietro said. "It is getting too dangerous for your mother . . . Anna go to the kitchen and get yourself a cup of coffee to relax and I will join you in a moment."

Anna was sitting in the kitchen having a cup of coffee wondering where the container and metal box were hidden. "Where did you bury the items," she asked her husband.

"Well, if I tell you then the fun will be over. See if you can find it."

After Anna finished her coffee, she went outside to find the container. Anna knew it was near the barn and started looking for signs of loose dirt or hay. She continued to look on both sides of the barn and in the back but couldn't see anything. *They couldn't have gotten too far from the house*, she thought. After about thirty minutes of searching she was about to give up. Anna was getting tired and walked over to the hazelnut trees next to the fields and sat down on one of the old chairs that they leave there for people to sit and enjoy the nuts. The trees had been there for as long as Anna could remember and they always had hazelnuts to eat year round. As she looked back at the main house, she could see Pietro and Bruno looking at her and smiling.

"You two look guilty of something," she yelled back at them.

"Do you give up, my dear?" asked Pietro.

Anna looked at her men. "Of course not, but if you two want dinner tonight you better tell me soon or you will be getting the kids from school and cooking us dinner."

They both started to laugh at the same time. Pietro finished smoking his pipe and tapping it on the bottom of his shoes and then placed it in his tobacco pouch he kept with him at all times. He walked to where Anna had sat down and placed both of his hands on her shoulders. She raised her head and looked into her husband eyes and said, "So where is the container?"

"You're sitting on top of it right now!" She looked down at the ground and didn't notice anything different about the appearance of the whole area. "It was Bruno's idea to bury it here with the trees and not near the barn or house because that is where they will be looking for food. They won't be looking for food where there is always food." She looked at the hazelnut tree, then at Pietro and Bruno, and all three started to laugh.

Chapter 4

BACK TO WAR

IT WAS FEBRUARY 1940 and the whole country was in turmoil. The direction in which Mussolini had played the country was starting to wear on its citizens and the world, mostly because of the cruelty that Germany was inflicting on countries that it invaded. The fact that Italy was part of the Axis Powers only hurt the country's efforts to get the world to support their expansion of power. The country still was not out of their financial problems, and to make matters worse jobs were still hard to find. Italy's future did not look promising and this also meant that its armed forces were struggling.

Catherina was getting ready to go see Gino at the hospital and was making her bed before she went to the kitchen to share a cup of coffee with Patricia. This was her routine since coming to Treviso months ago. As she made her way to the kitchen she couldn't help but wonder what was in store for Gino and, of course, their future as a married couple. He had gotten all of his strength back and the doctors had cleared him for full duty, but he was still awaiting orders from the army.

Gino's birthday was February 14, and Catherina needed to get him a present, but she was running low on funds. Bruno came to visit a couple of weeks ago and brought her some money plus wedding gifts from her parents. She noticed that Bruno still looked sick and wasn't very strong, but he explained that he started to work on the railroad lines plus working long hours had made him tired. As Catherina entered the kitchen, Patricia was already sitting at the dining room table with her coffee and morning smile. By the time Catherina made it down to the kitchen in the morning Patricia's husband and his parents were already gone for the day. Catherina always waited for them to leave before going to the kitchen so she wasn't a burden on their family.

"Good morning, Catherina, how did you sleep last night?" asked Patricia.

"Not so good I am sad to say. I am worried that Gino will be shipped off to some foreign land to fight another useless battle for expansion."

"When does he find out what his future is with the army?" Patricia asked.

"Soon they will clear him for duty and we are waiting for the army to send someone to tell him what his next assignment will be. It should happen this week."

"It has been very nice having you here," Patricia said. "I finally have someone my own age. Most of my days I don't get to have someone around that I can talk with, so you are welcome here for as long as you need to stay here in Treviso."

Catherina thanked her for the kind words and remarked that as soon as Gino left the hospital she would be returning to Cimpello and the farm. She would wait for him there until he returned from his time in the army. Patricia understood and excused herself from the kitchen so she could go to the markets and get some supplies. Catherina finished her coffee and dressed for the walk back to the hospital.

＊

As Catherina entered the hospital she noticed a couple of army trucks parked in front. When this happened they usually were retrieving the wounded being discharged. As she entered Gino's floor, she sensed something was going on as she passed the nurse's station. Nurse Trisha was going over some patient files with an army doctor. Catherina made her way to Gino's room and he wasn't alone; there was another soldier in his room with some boxes. Gino was putting on a uniform. Catherina walked up to Gino's bed.

"Gino, what is going on?" asked Catherina.

"They have decided that they need me for further service and are taking me today," replied Gino.

"For how long? Where are you going?" asked Catherina.

"That is for the upper command to decide," one of the soldiers interjected. "We are here only to gather soldiers that have recovered from their wounds. We are going to all the hospitals on this coast to pick up our soldiers. We have three to pick up from this hospital today."

Catherina looked at her husband with disappointed eyes. Gino was about to put his shoes on when he asked the soldier to leave the room so he could have some alone time with his wife. The soldier nodded and stood in the hallway.

"I was just paid. Take all the money and use it as you need. I will try and finish my tour as quickly as I can and return to Cimpello very soon."

"Can I stay with you until you leave?" asked Catherina.

"Of course you can. They still have to get the other two soldiers before we load up and leave for the truck," replied Gino.

Catherina escorted her husband to the truck with all the other soldiers and their families. She really was going to miss her husband and wanted to go with him. She knew he had no choice because desertion was punishable by death.

As they loaded up on the truck, Gino gave Catherina a long kiss goodbye and whispered into her ear that he would return soon and that he loved her. She stayed until the truck was out of sight and then walked back to Patricia's house to tell her the news that she was going back to Cimpello.

***

The train ride back to Cimpello went by quickly. As she arrived, Catherina noticed the changes in town right away. Bruno had told her what was happening when he visited her the last time in Treviso, but to see the Fascists with her own eyes was frightening.

Catherina's return was unannounced. Nobody came to meet her, so she had to walk home in the cold, which gave her time to

clear her head. There was so much to tell her mother and father
when she got back to the farm. She had missed her family and
wanted to see everyone again, but she knew things would be
different now that she was married.

Catherina made her way out of the town and towards the
farm before anybody noticed her. If anybody stopped her, she
wasn't even sure what to do or what to say so she just kept her
head down and walked very briskly. As she made her way to
the dirt roads towards the farming communities, one person
that recognized her noticed her from afar. Betty was sipping her
morning coffee. She knew who it was right away and became very
agitated as soon as she made the connection. Francisco would
be coming over for dinner tonight and Betty would tell him that
Catherina was back from Treviso. He couldn't resist looking for
contraband from people just arriving from other cities and this
would be a good reason for him to visit the Zucchet farm.

Francisco was recently appointed Adjunct Deputy
Commander, responsible for enforcing Fascist Italy's radical and
racial laws. One of his duties was to investigate all suspicious
activities and report them to the higher authority. Another one
of his duties was to submit all known Jewish families names
and what type of work they did in the community to his German
supporters. He disliked this duty and currently hadn't submitted
any names, even after his uncle told him to do so during his last
visit. There were rumors about what was happening to German
and Polish Jews after they were taken away, and he didn't want
that to happen to his fellow citizens here in Cimpello. He was
also assigned to collect all the extra metal and any other type
of material that the Italian and German Army asked for from
all the businesses, homes, and farms in Cimpello. Most of the
metal and other materials were needed to make ammunition
and other military gear for the ongoing war. The army sent
trucks and infantry weekly to collect all the material that was
collected, and Francisco always made sure that the trucks left
with as much material as they could carry. This, of course, was
possible because of all the pillaging that he and his supporters
did on a daily basis.

As Catherina made her way towards the farm, she could see
that things had changed since she left to take care of Gino. The

landscape looked different and the farms seemed to be missing some of their equipment. She also noticed that the amount of cattle outside feeding was fewer than she remembered. As she turned to start the always familiar walk on the cobblestone driveway, she noticed her mother outside hanging clothes to the left of the main house. It was a sunny day and not too cold and yet windy enough to dry clothes. Catherina knew her mother would be doing some type of laundry and, sure enough, there she was hanging up sheets to dry out.

"Momma," she cried out to Anna.

Anna stopped and yelled out for Pietro and at the same time started to run towards her eldest daughter. Pietro was not too far from the main house front door when he heard his name, so he made his way outside and saw what all the commotion was about. He saw Anna hugging Catherina.

"Welcome back, Catherina, we have missed you so much," Pietro said, hugging his daughter. "How is Gino doing?"

Catherina looked at her father and mother with tears in her eyes and said, "Just as he was totally recovering from his wounds, they came and took him away yesterday for further service. I don't know where they were taking him, but they were going to all the hospitals and taking all the military men who had recovered from their wounds."

"That means that they are hurting for men to fight and have started to round up all their wounded that have healed," Pietro said. "We are starting to see some changes here as well. Please help your mother finish with the sheets and we will tell you what is going on here in Cimpello."

As Catherina entered the house she noticed right away that certain items were missing from the main room and the kitchen was bare. Most of the kitchen pots, pans, and utensils that her mother had displayed were missing along with the sewing machine, large containers, and some other furniture pieces.

"Where is all of your kitchen items and furniture?" asked Catherina.

"The government has taken most of the items, but we also have hidden some so we will have them later," Pietro said.

"They just can't come here and take what they want, can they?" asked Catherina.

Pietro looked at his daughter and put her face into his hands. "Yes, they can take what they want as long as they let us keep what we need to survive. We only have one bull, one cow, one horse, and only half of the chickens that we used to have. All the goats are gone and so are the pigs."

Catherina sat and started to cry because she knew this wasn't good for the farm. Pietro sat next to his eldest daughter with a smile and placed a hand on her shoulder. "Why are you crying, my dear? We will be just fine; we have taken some measures to ensure our survival during this period of uncertainty."

"Like what, Dad? How are we going to survive without our animals?"

He looked at his daughter for some time and let her get all of her emotions out of her system. Anna was going about her business of getting the meals ready when Valerie and Velasco walked into the kitchen to welcome their oldest sister back home from her extended leave. As she was hugging her sister and brother, Pietro got up from his chair and walked next to his wife and gave her a glance. Pietro cleared his throat and told his two youngest to go get their jackets and go outside and play because he wanted to talk with Catherina. He would call them in when he was finished. Catherina was hugging both of her siblings and told them both that when they came back into the house she had some presents for them from Treviso.

"What do you want to tell me, Father?" said Catherina.

"While you were gone some things have changed around here and you will be a big help shortly, and you need to know what is going on in order to make sure this farm stays running in case something happens to your mother or me. First things first, my mother has moved into your room upstairs and will be living with us for some time. She has lost her ability to walk from her old age and not being very healthy. Her apartment in town is vacant right now and we are trying to sell it. You will need to help your mother take care of her and the duties you had before you went to help Gino. Also, we are working with the Martins, Manzon, and Pelliccia farms to produce different crops each year so that we can support one another throughout the year. We are not too sure what will happen, but we want to prepare for the worst in case they start taking more than what we produce. They have already taken a lot of livestock and probably will be coming back for more. Your brother Bruno is working for the railroad company again and is helping us with any extra money he makes from the job. He also helped me hide some pots around the farm to hide food and I will show you where we have hidden them. We also have made some modifications to the house and hid all our valuables. We took the liberty of hiding all of your jewelry you left here. The Fascists haven't started to take the valuables yet, but it is only a matter of time before they will start to need more money. Your mother is wearing a cheaper wedding band and I don't wear mine anymore. We also went to the bank and withdrew a lot of coins and have them hidden in the house as well. If anybody asks you, we gave the coins to you and Gino for your wedding present. You cannot tell anybody about all that I have told you, especially your friends and your younger sister and brother. They don't understand that they can jeopardize this family and farm's future. Do you have any questions?"

Catherina looked at her dad with a stunned look and began to look around the kitchen again; she just couldn't get used to looking at an empty kitchen.

"Dad, for how long will this last?" asked Catherina.

"I don't know, my dear, and you also need to know that Gino's father is not doing very well. He was hit in the head with a gun by the Germans a while back and hasn't been seen since. We think he is at his home recovering but we haven't been able to confirm his condition."

Catherina got up from the kitchen table and walked up to the kitchen sink to look out the window behind the sink. She could see her mother and her youngest siblings playing in the fields.

"Dad, I have no questions and will do everything I can do make sure this farm and this family survives. I will go see grandma now and move my stuff into Bruno's room."

Chapter 5

NAZIS ARRIVE

IN THE SPRING OF 1940, the Fascist movement in Italy had taken over just about all government programs and their assets. Mussolini and his supporters were running the country, but there were hidden movements that wanted to topple his reign. Most were disorganized, but a few were starting to get more support as the Fascists supporters continued pillaging and supporting Germany.

Catherina was helping her mother prepare dinner when she heard Bruno ride up on his bike. He was back from working the railroad job to help his father in the fields. It was planting season, which meant that most workers left their jobs to help out on their family farms. It was different this year than it had been in the past when it came to leaving the railroad and going back to work on the farm. Bruno almost didn't get to come home. The Fascists almost shipped him to go to work elsewhere in the country, but he wasn't in good health and avoided the unpaid transfer to get home in time for spring planting.

Bruno came into the kitchen with a grin. "Hmm, looks like someone has a letter from Naples." Catherina turned around from the sink and smiled at Bruno who was handing her the letter and giving his mother some supplies that she asked for him to pick up from his visit to the town. Anna looked at the vegetables and fruits that Bruno handed to her.

"This is all they had at the market, Bruno?"

"No, Mom, there were no vegetables or fruit at the market. I had to go see some friends to get what you see here. The Fascists take anything they want from the markets; so most people are not even going there anymore. It is very sad, and the only reason to go to town is to see some of my friends and find out the latest news."

Just then Pietro walked into the house from working the fields and saw Bruno. "What is the news for today, my son?"

"Not much news today, Dad, just the same stuff as the other day I went to town. Ever since they took over the newspapers, you really can't believe anything that you read. I talked with some of my friends and they are getting stripped of anything in their houses that even remotely looks like metal. I saw them going into the town hall and taking the chairs, desks, and file cabinets to give to the army. Francisco was there, as usual, telling everyone what to do and where to go next; he is such an idiot. Doesn't he know that when this is all over he isn't going to come out smelling very good for either side, especially if the Allies get a hold of him and his goon supporters?"

Pietro smiled at his son and put his hand on his shoulder for reassurance. He then noticed his daughter opening up a letter.

"So, what kind of news does Gino have about his next assignment?"

Catherina was reading the letter not even hearing her father's remarks. Gino was still in Naples being evaluated for further service. He hadn't done well enough when they looked at him months ago and they were monitoring his progress. He wasn't doing well, and from his letter it sounded like he still wasn't passing the physical fitness examinations.

"What does the letter say, Catherina?" asked Pietro.

"Nothing has changed, same situation as the last letter. They won't release him anytime soon but he isn't getting better. He says he still has problems breathing and can't catch his breath after doing minor labor tasks. They have him working at the hospital until they figure out what to do with him."

Catherina wasn't feeling too well and knew what was going on but didn't want to bother her mother and father with the news. She went back to helping her mother in the kitchen and put the letter in the pocket of her dress.

Bruno and Pietro went outside to sit and talk about the near future of the Zucchet farm. Pietro could see the fields that seemed to last forever. It was almost time to start getting the plow ready. It needed the annual sharpening and the harness needed mending from last year's crops. He also needed to start to feed the horse and cows more often so they would have the energy to pull the plow; with only three animals to pull the plow Pietro worried that they wouldn't be able to complete the planting.

Pietro looked at Bruno and noticed that he always looked so sick and weak, but he had always looked that way even as a child.

"What are you smiling about, Father?" asked Bruno.

"Well, your mother and I think your sister is pregnant and are wondering when she will tell us. She has gained some weight and seems to be sick every morning."

Bruno started to laugh. "That means you are going to be a grandfather and I am going to be an uncle. Well I guess we better plant more seed this year since we are going to have to feed more people in the future."

Pietro mentioned to Bruno that the farmers would be having another meeting that week and that he needed to be there. Then both of them saw the dust from the road, which meant that some vehicles were heading in their direction. They both looked to see if it was moving fast or slow. Slow moving dust usually meant it was horses, but fast moving dust meant some type of motor vehicle. Only the Fascists or Nazis owned motor vehicles in this part of Italy. It was fast-moving dust and they both went inside the house to prepare for the worst.

"They are coming. We need to get ready for them," yelled Bruno as he entered the house.

Anna and Catherina made all the preparations in the kitchen and Bruno gathered the children in the main room in the house. Pietro's mother was bedridden and couldn't leave the upstairs bedroom. Just as everyone got into their places, Pietro was looking through the window to see if they would make the left into the driveway of the farm. Even if they didn't make the left, they could always come back from the other farms down the road, but they usually stopped at the Zucchet farm first during their raids.

The dust was getting closer and Pietro was looking out the window when Bruno yelled, "We are ready, Dad."

Pietro nodded his head. *This is starting to get old*, he thought. The Zucchet family had made preparations for these events for some time now and they all knew their places and what to do during a raid. The first rule was always to give them what they want; the second rule was that only Pietro talked to them; finally, never tell them where they keep the food.

Pietro noticed that there were two vehicles making the turn to the farm. The first was the usual vehicle driven by Francisco's goons, but the second was a German vehicle.

"Why are the Germans coming out here?" Bruno whispered to his father. Pietro just shrugged his shoulders.

Both vehicles stopped just in front of the main house. Francisco made his way to the German sedan to let someone out. The German soldier looked like an officer of some type and he walked like he was far superior to anyone else. Pietro could see that Francisco was very nervous around this German officer and walked very close to him as they approached Pietro and Bruno.

"Mr. Zucchet, let me introduce you to our friend from the north, Major Klein. He doesn't speak Italian so I will be the translator."

Bruno always thought that was the reason Francisco was where he was because he could speak German; it sure wasn't his ability to get things done. Pietro looked at the officer and noticed that everything about his uniform was perfect; in fact it was too perfect. *Never trust someone who looks too good to be true.* Those were the words Pietro's father always used to say to him when he was growing up. The officer was looking at the fields as though they belonged to him, and he started to walk towards the barn that was behind the main house. Francisco followed. Pietro and Bruno did not move from the front of the house; they knew what was important to them and it was in the house. Francisco turned and was making waving motions at Pietro to come with them. Francisco and Major Klein stopped in front of the barn for a moment to let Pietro catch up to them.

Pietro smiled and said, "So what does he want from me, Francisco? We are only a small family farm barely able to feed our family, and we make just a little money for our next planting season. You have already taken just about everything we had that was extra and only allow us enough cooking and farming supplies to barely survive. When are we going to get some type of compensation that you promised when you were taking all of our metal and precious jewelry?"

"Your compensation will come soon enough," Francisco said. "An Italian invasion is planned and then we will be able to pay off our debt to you and everyone else who contributed to the cause."

Major Klein made a comment to Francisco and he turned in the direction of the hazelnut trees. The major smiled and started to clap his hands while he walked towards the trees. Bruno was watching from the house and started to panic. As they reached the trees, Francisco was smiling and remarked to Pietro that the major grew up on a farm that had hazelnuts on it and always enjoyed them.

"Well then he should take some before he leaves," Pietro said.

Major Klein grabbed a handful of nuts from the bucket and took a seat near the base of the tree. He looked at Francisco and Pietro and asked them to join him. Pietro could tell right away that the major was a veteran at opening these nuts. The major grabbed two nuts at a time and used one to open the other.

"So what crops will you be planting this year, Farmer Zucchet?" asked the Major.

Francisco translated the question and Pietro answered, "Beans, Major."

"So how many people can you feed with your beans?" Francisco asked for the major.

"Enough to feed Cimpello for a whole year, Major." The major started to laugh and continued to eat the hazelnuts.

Catherina was looking out the kitchen window with Anna and they both were shaking a little.

"What do you think they are talking about?" asked Catherina.

"I don't know, but your father is having a good time. I can tell by his body language. If Francisco and the German only knew what he was sitting on," she remarked. They both started to laugh.

"I am sure it is about the farm and what we can do for the Fascist and German armies. As long as there is conflict and wars they will always need farmers to feed their troops," remarked Anna.

Catherina was holding her stomach trying not to let the pain bother her or be noticed by her mother. There was so much going on with the farm that she didn't want to add to their problems. She was hoping that Gino would come home and be able to take her and the baby she was carrying somewhere and give the farm a break from all the people. There were a total of seven people living on the farm and it was already very crowded, but that never bothered Pietro or Anna because family always came first. Catherina had always remembered what her father would always say, "We always have room for family!"

Major Klein got up from the chair and took a couple of hand full of nuts and put them in his pockets. Then he started to walk towards the cars and about halfway stopped and turned to Pietro.

"You need to start producing more crops that would feed not only Cimpello but a whole battalion as well. That means twice as much as you are producing now." Pietro looked at the major and then at Francisco.

"This farm has been in my family for over ninety years, and we can only produce what we plant. If you and the government want more beans then you will have to give me more seed to plant. I only have enough seed from last year's crop to produce what we normally grow."

Pietro knew he had enough seed to do what they wanted. *But why not ask for more?* He would have to do double the work for less return. Francisco translated Pietro's concerns about not having enough seed to Major Klein who told Francisco that the Italian Agricultural Department had additional seed to give to the farmers. If Italy didn't have enough seed he would see if Germany would supply some.

Pietro wanted to alert other farmers right away about the major's demands and offer to provide seed so they could take advantage of this great opportunity.

Before the major pulled away he instructed his driver to fill up a potato sack with hazelnuts. Bruno immediately headed towards the driver to stop him from collecting all of the nuts. Pietro got in front of his son and grabbed him by his right upper arm and with one quick look into his sons eyes, Bruno stood down. Major Klein and Francisco observed what had occurred between Pietro and Bruno but did not say anything. The driver approached the trees and bent down, filling the bag with as many nuts as he could. He even emptied the bucket near the chairs.

The driver was getting close to where the container of food was buried. Catherina watched nervously, as did the others in her family.

"I am going outside to see what is going on with the Germans," she said to her mother.

"Be careful, my dear, and stay close to your father. Take the water container and some glasses for our visitors."

Catherina took the tray and some drinking glasses and headed for the main door.

The driver looked up and saw the very beautiful Italian woman with refreshments coming out of the house. The driver thought, *I am not going to collect any more of these hazelnuts while those other bastards sit around and look at that beautiful woman and drink something cold. I am done doing this ridiculous order from the major*. The driver picked up the bag full of nuts and started to walk towards Catherina.

Major Klein immediately pushed his way past Francisco to meet this very pretty young lady and get some refreshments from her. *It's amazing how one very beautiful woman could change a whole situation*, thought Francisco who was smiling now. He missed seeing Catherina in town and was very excited to see her again. Even though he didn't show it, Pietro was mad at his daughter for coming outside with the refreshments. It meant that they were staying longer and Pietro wanted them gone as quickly as they arrived.

"Major Klein, this is my daughter Catherina, she lives on the farm with us," replied Pietro. The major was already getting a glass of water from Catherina during the introductions. Bruno moved to the right so that the goons and the driver could get to their water, and at the same time Pietro moved in closer to his daughter to make sure nothing happened to her. The major smiled at Catherina and thanked her for the water.

"So, Mr. Zucchet, how many other people live on the farm other than your very pretty daughter?" asked the major. Pietro looked at the major and was about to answer his question when Francisco interrupted and answered him in German.

"Mr. Zucchet has a total of seven people living on the farm. His mother, wife, and another son and daughter also live on the farm."

Major Klein turned and looked at Francisco and immediately noticed the connection. "Do you two know each other?"

"Yes, I have known this family my entire life, Major. They are one of the best farmers in the region."

"Well if Francisco thinks you are one of the best farmers I will have to take his word for it and come and visit more often. Besides, I will need to get more hazelnuts when I run out. Thank you for your refreshments, Mr. Zucchet, and have a good day."

The major's car pulled out first as their entourage continued down the road towards the other farmers and the big estate of the local count, who owned a large parcel of land.

"I was afraid that the driver was going to see the wooden door to the food," Catherina said. "He wasn't just picking up the nuts; it seemed that he was digging at the same time trying to get to the nuts under the ground."

Bruno ran over to the area that she was talking about and there it was, the wooden access panel. How the driver missed it was anybody's guess. Bruno would have to make it deeper and harder to get to the access panel. It would be done that night in the cover of darkness. He pretended to pick up a couple of nuts just to distract anybody's curiosity.

Pietro walked next to his daughter and said, "I was worried about the driver as well and he did get really close. Good thinking coming out here with the water. Was that your idea or your mother's?"

"It was both of our idea. Great women come up with great ideas."

As Catherina entered the house, Pietro stopped to speak with his son.

"Bruno, you need to keep your cool around the Germans

and Fascists or something bad is going to happen to you, or to us. Do you understand?" Bruno looked at his father with disappointment in his eyes and nodded.

"Do you want to be in the same situation as Gino's father?"

Bruno was now getting upset with his father and lashed out. "Dad, those people just come on our farm and take what they want and just leave like they own this farm. Where are the police or army to stop them? Why don't you stop them?" asked Bruno.

Pietro took a deep breath. "Listen, this is going to last for a long time just like War World I, so we need to be patient and take care of this farm and family the best we can. If we fight the Germans or the Fascists we will lose. Now I need you to go to the Martins, Manzon, and Pelliccia farms and tell them about how we are getting more seeds from the Fascist and Germans and that they should tell them they don't have enough seed as well. Also, tell them that if they haven't started to hide food, they need to start as soon as possible."

Bruno went to the barn and took off on his new motorcycle to tell the other farmers what had taken place at their farm that day. He was very proud of the motorcycle that he had bought from the money he had saved over the years working with the railroad company.

***

Catherina was in the kitchen cleaning the glasses and pitcher from their visitors when Pietro walked into the room. He stood next to his daughter and gave her a kiss on the cheek and put his right hand over her stomach.

"When are you going to tell us that you are expecting?"

"Pietro, don't you have something else to do other than harass our daughter about the new addition to our family," Anna scolded. "We were just talking about what the new living arrangements will be when you walked into the kitchen. Go take the children outside for some fresh air."

Pietro looked at Anna, took a deep breath, mumbled something under his breath, and then he walked to the back door with Valerie and Velasco. Catherina and Anna said nothing to each other until Pietro and the children left the house. Anna took her daughter's left hand with her right hand, moving her away from the kitchen counter, and then took her left hand and put it on her stomach while at the same time looking into her oldest daughter's eyes with the biggest smile, and then she hugged her.

"We are going to have a baby!"

Chapter 6

Maria Arrives

BY THE FALL OF 1940, Germany had already taken over France and were attacking England. Italy had joined the war in June, but only because Mussolini was afraid that Germany would get all the rewards of the war. So Mussolini ordered his troops to attack his nearest rival geographically, which was France, who surrendered to Germany in mid-June. This invasion grabbed a small piece of land but the French put up a fierce resistance, and a full-scale invasion of southern France never occurred. In September, Mussolini gave another order to attack the British troops based in Egypt. This was the start of a war that was to be disastrous for Italy and caused Mussolini to lose support.

After the invasions of France and Egypt, the Italian government made it very difficult for individuals to leave military service. The only real strength that Italy had was that their army was one of the largest, with over a million troops. But what most outsiders were unaware of was their lack of heavy equipment support, which was very vital in modern warfare. This meant that any chance of Gino returning home was not going to happen anytime soon.

During this period, most of the farmers in Northern Italy were left to their crops, but the pillaging and harassment by the

Fascists and Germans continued. Additionally, the call for all Jewish family names to be reported to the Fascist supporters and then turned over to the Germans gained momentum. Although most families in Northern Italy did not have Jewish names, the threat of turning their names over always produced positive outcomes for the Fascists.

The Zucchet family was enjoying one of their best crops in recent memory and celebrating the birth of Catherina and Gino's daughter, Maria. Bruno was still at the farm but his health was starting to affect his ability to do work. He struggled to keep any weight on his body. Bruno wasn't travelling in town as much for the fear that they would take him into the army or the Fascist party. His mother had suspected that when he last went to work with the railroad company he contracted tuberculosis, but she kept that information to herself and wasn't about to let the other family members in on her theory. Just to be safe, they had Bruno move to the other side of the house to prevent him from infecting the others. All the other members of the family continued to be healthy.

The other farmers in the region were not as lucky as the Zucchet farm. Pietro would venture into the town to catch up on the news about once a week. Pietro was doing more traveling than in the past, but he didn't mind. It allowed him to stay up with the news and see what the other farmers were doing in the region. During one of his visits, he learned that the most notable farm in the region that was affected by the recent visits from the Fascists and Germans was the farm owned by the Italian royal family. The farm was on the east side of the Zucchet farm and was a very large plot of land. The rumor in Cimpello was that the royal family refused to supply the Fascists and Germans with food. The Germans shut the farm down, sending those working it away.

The Zucchet farm was mostly one plot of land and it was this parcel that most of the locals knew about, but Pietro also owned a plot of land just on the other side of the Italian royal family farm. Since the visit by Francisco and Major Klein, the Zucchet farm needed to produce more crops, which meant that this plot was needed for planting. In the past, it was mostly used for grazing of the animals.

During the summer planting season, Pietro and Bruno were constant travelers on the main road to their extra plot of land. This gave them a perfect view of the main farmhouse and of the royal farm. Pietro noticed that there wasn't much activity at the farm throughout the summer and he knew he needed to keep his distance for there was a very successful movement to disestablish the royal authority by the Fascists and Germans. Pietro didn't want to be known as anybody's supporter.

Although the Fascists and Germans were seen more often than in the past, their visits to the Zucchet farm were not as frequent. With the exception of the seed drop off and one other visit by Francisco, everyone stayed away. The only concern for Pietro was that after Francisco's visit, he left very angry after finding out that Catherina was pregnant and married to Gino.

The royal farm had largely been abandoned. The plot of land that was usually full of corn, beans, or other crop was not planted or being attended. Pietro knew what was going on and warned the other farmers during the gatherings to stay clear of the royal farm for the fear of being guilty by association. By the end of September, the royal farm looked deserted and pillaged. Pietro could see that the caretaker was still living at the main house as smoke came out of the chimney most of the evenings.

During the early part of October, Pietro was settling down one evening with Anna and his youngest son and daughter. Catherina was in the main house feeding Maria before putting her down for the evening. Anna had brought his evening cup of coffee to him while he was smoking his pipe. His son was chasing his daughter through the chickens near the north side of the main house near the barn when they all heard the loud noise coming from the royal farm. Pietro immediately recognized the sound and told Anna, who was already moving in the direction of her two youngest, to get the children inside the house. Pietro sat calmly and smoked his pipe as he noticed the Fascist cars go by his farm. Francisco was sitting in the back of the sedan with his uncle as they drove by. At that moment, Pietro realized that no matter what the future held for this family and his country it wasn't going to be easy, and there was another war getting ready to start in Italy. Pietro called out to Bruno.

"Was that a gunshot we heard?" Bruno asked.

Pietro nodded. "It was a pistol shot we heard."

Anna and Catherina looked at each other in horror and shock. "What are we going to do now?" asked Catherina.

"We are not going to do anything until it gets dark. Then Bruno and I will go see if something has happened," Pietro said.

Pietro finished his coffee and cigar while Bruno went to the barn and brought out two bikes. His father didn't want to make any noise to attract attention so he told Bruno to be quiet when getting the bikes ready. When Bruno finished bringing the second bike to the side of the house, Pietro told Bruno to go get a shovel and a lamp from the barn and bring it with them.

At midnight Pietro went and got Bruno up from his deep sleep. They made their way to the royal farm using the bikes, with Bruno carrying the shovel and Pietro carrying the lamp. As they went down the main road, Pietro looked up to see all the stars and the half-moon in the sky and he knew that what they were about to find wasn't going to be good. Based on his experience in the past war, he knew that pistols were never used unless there was close combat or for executions.

As they came off the main road and started down the side road to the royal main house, there was no smoke coming out of the house and it was very still. Pietro could see something on the ground. As they got closer, he noticed that there was blood. Pietro looked at his son and put his finger to his mouth. "Be quiet; we don't want anybody noticing us here."

***

Catherina was getting Maria ready for bedtime when Anna came to her room with a letter from Gino. Pietro had made a run into town earlier that day and stopped by to get the mail. He also stopped by to read the latest news that was posted in the town center. Pietro was very concerned with what he had learned during this trip to Cimpello. First, the Italians attacked the British in Egypt and the Germans were starting to move more soldiers into Italy. *This is worse than World War I*, thought Pietro, after sitting in front of the farm at his usual bench waiting for Bruno.

The weather was getting colder; the fields were in need of one more turning before the winter set in.

"We need to turn the ground one more time before the ground gets too hard. Tomorrow should be the day when we start, and we could be finished in three days if we don't push the horses too much," Pietro said.

Bruno just looked at his father and shrugged apathetically.

Anna was in the kitchen washing dishes when Catherina entered with the baby.

"Mom, I have some great news about Gino. He is going to be transferred to Rome soon. That means he will be closer to us and will be able to come visit us real soon hopefully."

"Let's go find your father and tell him the great news," replied Anna.

Pietro heard the girls laughing in the kitchen, so he got up from his bench after putting his pipe down in the ashtray to see what was making his wife and daughter so happy.

Catherina was holding a letter, which meant there was good news about Gino. Anna saw her husband enter the kitchen.

"Gino is getting moved to Rome soon. Isn't that good news, Pietro?" asked Anna.

"Yes, that is good news. Does he say what he will be doing in Rome, Catherina?"

"He will be doing the same thing he did in Naples, working on electrical equipment, but he doesn't know exactly where in Rome as of yet," replied Catherina.

Pietro walked up next to Catherina and she exchanged hugs with her father. Pietro was feeling a moment of real joy for the first time in a long time, so he simply reached for Maria and took her from his daughter. He made his way into the main room of the house next to the main window and yelled the good news to Bruno. He sat down on the chair next to the window with Maria in his arms, covering his granddaughter with the blanket he took from the chair. As Bruno walked towards the back of the house, Pietro could see that his son looked like his was getting worse. He held Maria and wondered if she, or any family member, would survive the war.

The next day Pietro and Anna were in the barn getting ready for the meeting with all the other farmers. It was their turn this month but they had been doing it more often because the other farmers were having hard times. Anna set up the table with the usual food and drinks.

"Anna, what is going on in that mind of yours?" asked Pietro. She stopped and turned around to talk with Pietro so he could hear her better. He was getting older and was losing his hearing.

"I was just thinking how lucky I am for having such a smart farmer as a husband. You always seem to know what to do when we need you the most, and we are never without food," answered Anna.

"Well, honey, you help me figure out what to do most of the time and it probably was a good thing we didn't get that tractor a couple of years ago," answered Pietro.

The other farmers always looked at Pietro as an "old farmer" who didn't want to change his ways because his attitude was *if it works, don't fix it.* The other farmers were already using tractors, updated spades, and other mechanical advancements that made their crops more productive and they could produce more. The farmers were forced to go back to the old ways of farming by using just cattle, horses, hand picking crops, and a spade. Most of the farmers did not have the know-how or physical ability to go back to the old way of farming. Only the Zucchet and the Martin farms produced the same amount of crops as they did their previous year.

***

It was around seven o'clock when the farmers started to arrive at the Zucchet farm. Pietro went out to the driveway to greet everyone. The Martin's were always first; they only lived just a short walk to the farm. Then came the Manzon, and then, finally, the Pelliccia family arrived by horseback; their motor vehicles had been confiscated long ago. Not as many people attended the meeting as previous meetings and it was obvious this had to do with transportation. In the past, vehicles were available, but now only horses and cattle remained, making transporting large groups of people more difficult. The heads of each farm, which usually meant heated discussions about the future of farming, would only attend tonight's meeting.

Anna was leaving the barn, knowing that she could not be the only woman there, but she would get the minutes of the meeting from her husband just as all the other wives would get from their husbands. She noticed that Anthony Pelliccia was very distressed and not looking very healthy. *He deserves whatever is making him sick*, she thought. As Anna exited the barn and the door closed behind her, Pietro turned to the other farmers and looked at all three family heads. It was starting to get cold and the wind started to pick up; each one of them looked really tired and frustrated. Francisco really was causing a lot of problems for everyone, and there seemed to be no stopping him and the pillaging.

Pietro walked towards the table to get a glass of wine. Just as he grabbed his wine he heard Anthony speak.

"Pietro, thanks for having us over, but this is going to end soon. Francisco came over just the other day and told us that we should be getting our equipment back or some type of monetary settlement for the last year," replied Anthony.

Pietro looked at Anthony and then at the other two men who were both shaking their heads in disbelief.

"I can't believe you just said that, Anthony. Do you really believe anything that Francisco says to you? He is under the control of the Germans, and there is no way we are getting anything back. Have you taken steps to get ready for this winter yet?" asked Pietro.

"Yes, we have taken the necessary steps to survive this winter, but Francisco has been giving us the guidance that we need. He has assured us that we don't need to hide any of our food and that everything should be documented that we currently have on the farm so when we are given our severance next year they know exactly what is owed to us."

Pietro could not believe what he was hearing, and neither could Greg Martin and John Manzon. Pietro would not share any of his secrets with the other farmers; he knew that there was always a possibility that they would tell Francisco. He even thought that maybe Anthony was telling Francisco about the meetings. If that was true, he needed to find out, and the sooner the better.

"Well, Anthony, if you are right that would be great for all of us, but we should prepare for the worst and hope for the best," replied Pietro.

As the evening wore on most of the discussions were surrounding what was going on with the families and which crops were going in next spring. It was Pietro's turn to grow corn. He liked corn because it was easy to pick and didn't require a lot of attention like the other crops. As the meeting was wrapping up, Pietro was walking the farmers out and told Anthony to hold up until everyone was gone so he could talk to him.

"So, Anthony, if something happens this winter and you need some extra food, we stored some in my mother's apartment in town. Nobody would suspect hiding food in town—not even Francisco," Pietro said.

"That is very generous of you, Pietro, but we won't need any extra food this winter," replied Anthony.

"Very well. Please tell Gilda and your mother we said hello."

As Anthony rode off, Pietro went back to the barn to make sure that all the lanterns were shut off. Anna was already in the barn cleaning up when Pietro came back to the barn.

"So what was said this evening," she said. Pietro took a deep breath then took a sip of his wine and explained the whole evening to Catherina.

"Is he that gullible to think that Francisco will repay us," replied Catherina.

"He is not as worldly as most of us are, dear. All he knows is that farm and what his mother tells him to believe," Pietro said. "We have to make sure the apartment is ready to go in case he is telling Francisco what we are saying in the meetings. I will go check the apartment tomorrow and make sure there isn't any food in there, and just some old furniture that they can take," Pietro said.

***

Pietro got up early the next morning so he could get into town and check the apartment. As he left the house, Catherina was already up feeding Maria and Anna was getting something from the kitchen. He kissed her and told her that he would be back late that afternoon from his run to town. Pietro would be making some stops along the way, including checking on some other farmers, stopping to read the news, going by the auction house, and, of course, the apartment.

By the time Pietro arrived in Cimpello it was already late morning. He had already looked at the other farms during his bike ride to town. There wasn't anything unusual about the town when he arrived, in fact, it looked more quiet than normal, so he decided to go into town and finish up his chores before leaving for home. He headed to the center of town to read the latest news and make sure that Chester's name wasn't on the wounded list. Chester hardly wrote letters home so it was hard to know where he was during this crazy war, but Pietro always checked to make sure he wasn't on the list. Last he heard from him he was overseas in Africa somewhere and he was not having the time of his life.

Pietro arrived at the center of town and there was nobody there but him. It wasn't that unusual to be the only one there but he did look around before stepping up to read the news. As he read through the paper and the list of the wounded or killed, he heard a car pull up and turned around to see Francisco. As he opened the door, out came Francisco looking like he was some type of movie star. Pietro remembered him as a spoiled little kid that always was crying about something or wanting something that he couldn't have, and now he was the town's Fascist leader who inflicted pain and misery when he thought it was necessary.

What has happened to our little town of Cimpello? thought Pietro. He noticed that Francisco started caring a gun and wearing gloves all the time. His uniform was getting more elaborate every time Pietro ran into him or he came to visit the farm. He was now wearing red epaulets, but Pietro didn't know what they meant or even cared. As Francisco approached Pietro, he knew it wasn't going to be a good meeting.

"So what brings you town, Pietro?" asked Francisco.

"Just catching up with the news and running by the auction house to see what is new," answered Pietro.

"So how is the family doing?" asked Francisco.

"We are doing just fine. Everyone is healthy and we are finishing up getting the farm ready for winter. Thank you for asking, Francisco, but if you would excuse me I have to make a couple more stops before I head home. I want to get home before the sun sets and it gets even colder," replied Pietro.

As Pietro started to walk away, he noticed that the driver and other Fascist thug were headed in his direction at the end of the steps. Pietro always thought he could take Francisco out, but not today. That would have to be another time or place.

"So, Pietro, how is your mother coming along?" asked Francisco.

"She is doing just fine, however, she is not walking around as much as she used to and pretty much stays upstairs. Thank you for asking, and how is your mother doing?" asked Pietro.

"She is fine and at home. So who lives in her apartment now?" asked Francisco.

"Well nobody lives there now. We are selling the apartment, but haven't had any luck right now," answered Pietro.

"How about we go over there and take a look at what is inside the apartment. We may need to take an inventory of what is in there for later use by the government," replied Francisco.

"Sure, I just happen to have the key with me," answered Pietro.

Pietro was heading to his bike and just as he was getting on it one of the thugs grabbed his arm. Pietro turned to the thug and just before he was going to punch him, Francisco said, "Pietro, why don't you just get into the car and we can make this faster. The bike will be here when we get back." Pietro remembered his family and how little Maria would need him in the coming years, so he quickly put the thoughts of violence away for now.

As they drove up to the apartment building, Pietro was looking out the right window to see if anybody was in the apartment or if there was any type of movement. He could see nothing and when he moved his vision back to the street ahead he noticed that Francisco was looking at the same window.

"Did you see something, Pietro?" asked Francisco.

"No, nothing looks different in the road or the back of the heads of our travel companions." Pietro knew that if he showed any type of fear Francisco could smell it and he would not get home tonight.

Pietro told the driver to stop at the entrance of the apartment building. It was an open-breeze apartment staircase that had no windows and it was three stories high. His mother lived on the third floor on the right corner of the building with a window facing the main road that they just drove up on. It was an older building but made out of concrete, so it was very sturdy but it needed a new outer coating of plaster. As they all exited the car, Pietro looked to the left of the building and could see the children playing in the open field. As soon as they all exited the car and started to approach the main staircase, he saw mothers racing for their children so they could take them to shelter.

Cimpello was under a storm of fear and obedience was the only cover for this storm. Nobody wanted to acknowledge that they knew Pietro for the fear of being an accomplice to whatever crime that they were investigating. Pietro realized that things would change after being escorted by these thugs of the government and he would take full advantage to seal his family's survival. Most of these folks had never been through rough times before and only made assumptions of what they saw and gossiped.

"I am surprised you didn't know where my mother lived, Francisco. Your grandmother and my mother were very good friends," remarked Pietro.

"I didn't get along with my grandmother, so we didn't talk much. So which apartment is it?" asked Francisco.

Pietro pointed to the upper right of the building and remarked, "It is the one on the upper right corner on the third floor. You can see how managing these steps could take the legs out of an old woman."

"Let's go see what is inside. I have other affairs to attend to and don't want to be bothered with this farmer stuff anymore today," remarked Francisco.

Pietro knew that Anthony had told him that he had hidden food in the apartment at this moment. Pietro always knew that someone was feeding Francisco information but couldn't put his finger on the person until now.

"Sure, let's go see this place. Are you interested in buying or renting? Is there someone in your family that needs a place? We could come up with an arrangement because of your new position as deputy. It has two bedrooms and one bathroom but not much furniture. We moved most of the furniture out to the farm but the government came and took most of that as you know," remarked Pietro as they walked upstairs.

Pietro could see that Francisco was getting angry the more he talked about the apartment, but he didn't want them to see any change in his demeanor. At just about the second story

Francisco grabbed Pietro's right elbow with enough force to stop Pietro's momentum and turn him around to face Francisco.

"Listen, I am not interested in buying this apartment and neither is the government, however, we are interested in what you may have hiding in it so stop talking and open the apartment," remarked Francisco.

Pietro was looking at Francisco talking and immediately noticed that his right hand was on his pistol. If the other two supporters were not with them, Pietro would have made short order of this situation. Pietro smiled at Francisco and apologized for any misunderstandings. As they approached the apartment, Pietro could hear door after door opening and shutting throughout the complex, and he wondered if the stories that his mother used to tell him about door signals were true. He always thought his mother was a little on the paranoid side, but maybe she was right. Pietro put the key in the door and unlocked the door. Francisco immediately pushed his way inside.

As Francisco passed Pietro, the other two supporters moved Pietro towards the center of the living room, which was on the other side of the apartment. Pietro started to look around the apartment and it was as if he was there just yesterday, nothing was missing and there was no food. He could hear Francisco looking around the apartment and noticed that one of the other supporters was in the kitchen and bathroom. All three of them smelled like some type of cleaning detergent. Pietro felt sick to his stomach because it reminded him of his earlier years.

Pietro could see down the hallway and noticed his mother's neighbor was looking out of her door. Pietro made a motion with his hand so that the neighbor would shut her door because he was worried that they would shift their attention on her apartment. He didn't stop smiling during the whole process and she complied without making any noise with her door.

"If you let me know what you're looking for I can help you find it, Francisco," remarked Pietro.

Pietro could see Francisco going from the master bedroom to the smaller bedroom moving furniture and anything else that was in the rooms. The other supporter yelled out that he found nothing but dust and dirt in the kitchen and bathroom. Francisco made his way to the main living room that everyone was standing in waiting for his next move. He looked to his left and could see a balcony, but even from that distance there was nothing to see. Francisco looked around the apartment one more time before returning to the living room.

"Does this place have a storage area in the basement?" asked Francisco.

"Why it sure does, would you like to see it?" remarked Pietro.

"Let's go see the storage area and what it has to offer us," remarked a smiling Francisco. As they made their way downstairs, Pietro could hear the doors opening and shutting again, it was some type of signaling system that they were using to tell each other what the Fascists were doing in the complex. As they made their way to the ground floor, Pietro continued down the stairs to the basement. He made his way to the storage cages and realized that this could be the best place to get killed and nobody could say they saw anything. For the first time since being picked up by this mob of thugs, Pietro was concerned for his safety so he positioned himself to make sure he would have a chance to survive.

His mother's storage area was the second one on the right, and because it was a cage they could see that there was nothing but dirt and dust and a couple of old empty wine containers.

"I need to come and get the two wine containers. We can use them on the farm, unless you want them, Francisco," remarked Pietro.

Pietro could feel the heat coming from Francisco's body. He started to back away from Francisco so as not to be too close but enough to block him into the other two thugs if needed. Francisco turned in the direction of Pietro and at the same time he seemed to have a sense of relief over his face.

"No, we don't need those wine containers. We are sorry that we bothered you, Pietro. Please tell Anna and Catherina I said hello. Let's go. I have other engagements I need to attend to before the end of the day."

As they walked away from Pietro, he stood there and didn't move an inch. He could hear them go up the stairs and out of the building complex and at the same time the doors started to open and shut again. Pietro started to smile and laugh as he heard the car drive away. As he started to walk away from the complex towards the center of town to retrieve his bike, he could hear the doors opening and shutting, which brought a smile on his face. *What a day*, he thought, and one that would change the way Pietro would feed the enemy.

Chapter 7

First Deserters

IN THE SPRING OF 1941, Italy was fighting in France, Africa, and Albania. Mussolini was trying to continue his quest to expand Italy's territories and keep up with Hitler's expansion as well. It was also during this period that Germany shifted its focus from Great Britain and onto Russia. The Italian Army was starting to show signs that it was unable to win battles and becoming more of a burden to Germany than an asset. Germany started to occupy more of Italy during this period with a special emphasis on Rome and other larger cities. The German occupation of Italy was seen as very hostile by most Italians, which made matters even harder on Mussolini and the Fascist supporters. The Axis Powers were also expanded when Yugoslavia joined Germany, Italy, and Japan. The Germans also gained more control of Italy's resources.

***

Pietro was sitting on the front porch of the farm looking out into the fields wondering where his son Chester was fighting or if he had been hurt. They hadn't heard from him in quite some time, but that never bothered Pietro because he remembered that when he was in the army he didn't write home very often. From the last letter they received his unit was going to be moved from Ethiopia and transferred up to Egypt to help the Germans fight the British. Pietro thought that all this fighting was a path of destruction for Italy. Pietro would always tell his family that Mussolini wasn't doing anybody any favors by trying to keep up with Germany.

It was getting warmer thought Pietro; he even was sitting with only a shirt on for the first time in months. He usually wore his sweater or a coat when he sat outside smoking his pipe. Maria was getting so big and she had started to crawl so there had been some changes around the farmhouse, but that only made Pietro smile knowing that he was a grandfather and that his Catherina was happy.

Pietro and Bruno needed to turn the ground over in the next couple of days, spread the cow manure, and get the seed ready for planting. It was about two when Pietro heard some noise outside in the driveway and when he went to investigate he found somebody had dropped off some extra corn seed for him to plant. He knew that he requested the seed, but didn't expect so much and wondered who dropped it off. When he compared the seed with his own, he noticed that the new seed was far more superior in size and texture. He wondered if the other farmers had received seed just as he did, but since the incident with Anthony telling Francisco about storing food, Pietro had not spoken with the other farmers. It had been at least four months since the incident and he didn't trust anybody except the Martins. But not even Gregory or his wife, Martina, knew about their hiding places or what was in them.

Pietro had sat down with everyone and explained what happened that day and how close he came to not making it home because of what Anthony had told Francisco. Pietro could only figure that Anthony wasn't producing the right amount of crops and was trying to divert attention from himself. Pietro wondered what happened to Anthony. Had Francisco punished him?

This was the time to relax before the spring planting season, and some farmers like the Zucchets took other jobs to supplement their incomes. Pietro worked the railroad just as Bruno did, but it had been years since he stopped working for the railroad and had no desire to go back. If Chester were home, he too would be asked by his father to find other work to help support the farm during the winter months just before the spring planting season. Even Anna and Catherina helped out with seamstress duties at the local silk factory when needed. But now that Catherina had Maria, only Anna would work at the silk factory when Valerie and Velasco were at school. It was the way of life for the farmers in this region.

Pietro got up from his familiar spot and started to move around his farm. He was looking at what needed to be done now that spring was around the corner. He noticed that the barn needed some cleaning up around the outside. During the winter months even he got a little lazy and didn't always clean up as he should. He entered the barn and grabbed his shotgun that was placed just inside of the door. It was warm and the rabbits would be running around the fields, which meant fresh meat for dinner. As he looked out to the fields, he could see the acres and acres of corn stalks that needed to be gathered and burned. They had done their job over the winter by stopping most of the soil erosion. The stalks also provided valuable nutrients that washed into the soil during the winter months, a natural fertilizer that cost nothing.

As he exited the barn, he noticed that he didn't have to kick or push the usual flock of chickens that gathered around his feet. Anna must have sold some and didn't tell him. Nobody could get a chicken ready for sale like his Anna. The chickens were not his prime source of income; the eggs were just as good as gold and as the war continued the eggs would be even more valuable. As Pietro walked the fields he noticed that the ground was getting warmer and the stalks of corn were generating heat. As he approached each stack, he would kick it to see what emerged from the center. Hopefully his reflexes would be fast enough to get a rabbit or two. He was about halfway through his major field when he noticed rabbit droppings. This was a good sign; they seemed to be to the left of the stack just in front of him. He checked his shotgun one more time to make sure it was ready and made his move to the stack. He kicked the stack and sure enough, a couple of adult rabbits came out running for their lives. Pietro got off one shot and was able to hit one of the rabbits as it darted to the right of the stack. He shot again and killed another. After he shot his gun, he heard what sounded like rustling in front of him and suspected it was more rabbits running away. As he was approaching one of the fallen rabbits, he noticed chicken feathers being blown around the corn stacks. He picked up the fallen rabbit and wondered how so many chicken feathers made it this far from the farm. Anna and Catherina were always great at keeping the feathers from flying away and collecting them for sale later on for pillows and mattresses at the farmers market.

He followed the trail of feathers to a corn stack at the very end of his field. He held up his shotgun not knowing what was in the stack but had a suspicion of who or what was inside. Pietro got closer to the corn stack, kicking it as he came to the base of the stack. He bent down to look inside and noticed some type of old, grey military clothing and pieces of dead chicken parts to the side. He also noticed a small fire pit, and then he heard a running noise coming from the main road just to the left of him. Two Italian soldiers ran from his farm towards the town of Cimpello.

Deserters, he thought. *Could this be a start of the Italian army's fall?* Pietro would need to have another meeting with the other farmers and see if they have seen what happened here today, but until then he needed to protect his farm and his family. He tore down the corn stack that the army guys occupied and cleaned up the area. He wanted to make sure nobody else would see this and think it was fine to pillage his farm.

Pietro came into the kitchen with the two rabbits. Anna came into the kitchen as Pietro was washing up at the kitchen sink. She knew something was wrong because he brought the shotgun into the kitchen. Anna hated guns and made it perfectly clear that he was not to bring them into the house unless he needed to protect the family. Pietro was wiping the water off from his face and turned to his wife who was looking at the rabbits and the shotgun on her kitchen table. He knew that the rabbits were not the problem.

"Anna, we had some visitors at the end of the farm and they killed some of our chickens," said Pietro. Anna didn't say anything but took both of the rabbits outside to skin them and get them ready for dinner. Pietro followed her; she sat down on her chair near a tree stump that had been there for years and one she used as a butchers table. He stood next to her and waited for her to say something. After about ten minutes she finally asked, "What are we going to do to prevent this from happening again? This farm will not last if the army comes through here and takes everything."

"Well the first thing I am going to go do is go to town and on my way to town I am going to stop by the Martin and Manzon farms and see if they have had this problem as well. If we do something now, it should stop future problems with the army. When I was in the army, if you stole food from a farmer you were punished very harshly and could have even been hanged."

***

Pietro went into Bruno's room and pounded on his door to wake him up. When he answered the door Pietro noticed that he looked like he had been out with friends drinking.

"What is going on?" asked Bruno.

"We had some army deserters that were living in the corn stacks eating our chickens. Have you heard of anybody else encountering or seeing army deserters in town or pillaging farmers?"

Bruno nodded.

"I am going to visit some of the other farmers and go to town to see if anybody else has been encountering deserters. I need you to watch the farm. The shotgun is in the kitchen and so is the ammo belt. I will be back by nightfall," replied Pietro.

"No problem, and you should go by the Pelliccia place because something is not right. They haven't been doing anything in preparation for the spring season and it looks as though it is deserted," replied Bruno.

Pietro was nearing the town of Cimpello on his bike at around two o'clock in the afternoon.

He had stopped by the other two farms and both had not seen any deserters, but they had been missing some of their livestock. The state usually compensated farmers if they could prove they had lost livestock from being pillaged, plundered, or killed accidently. Pietro made his way through the main street towards the main building of the old police station, which was now the headquarters of the Fascists supporters and their German allies. He parked his bike in front of the building and made his way to the front desk of the station. As he entered the building, he noticed that he wasn't alone in the lobby and that there were a few other people there to complain or to ask questions. He took his place in line and waited to be called. After about twenty minutes, he was called up to the clerk.

"What is your name," asked the clerk.

"My name is Pietro Zucchet, and I am a local farmer," replied Pietro. The clerk looked at Pietro and wrote down the information.

"What is your business with us today, Mr. Zucchet?" asked the supporter.

"I am here to let you know that I witnessed two army deserters pillaging from my farm," replied Pietro.

The clerk raised his head. "What did they take, Mr. Zucchet?" asked the clerk.

"Well when I was hunting, I saw them run away from the corn stack that they made into their temporary home with some of my chickens in their backpacks," replied Pietro.

"How many deserters did you see, Mr. Zucchet, and how many chickens did they kill?"

"I saw two running from my fields and three chickens were killed," replied Pietro.

The clerk was writing the information down and when he finished he got up from his chair and went into the back. Pietro waited for him to return and was looking around the lobby at all the folks waiting. He recognized most and the one thing he noticed was the look of desperation on everyone's face. The last time he had seen so many desperate faces was during the last war and this was just the start. The clerk returned and handed Pietro a voucher for the loss of the chickens. Pietro looked at the voucher and recognized it as the same worthless voucher he received for all the metal that they took from his farm, including Bruno's new motorcycle.

"What am I supposed to do with this voucher?" asked Pietro.

"You will receive the three chickens or their lira value when the local authority meets next week," replied the clerk.

"The other farmers in my region have been pillaged as well," replied Pietro.

"If the other farmers have been pillaged they need to

come make a claim and have evidence that this has happened to them. We know this happened to you because we have the two deserters in custody and they had your chickens in their backpacks," replied the clerk.

"What will happen to the young men?" asked Pietro.

"That is up to the local authority next week. You can come and see for yourself when they talk about your case," replied the clerk.

Pietro picked up the voucher and walked out to his bike. He got on his bike and started to shake uncontrollably when he realized that he could have just sent both deserters to their deaths for stealing his chickens, but it soon passed because he knew desertion was probably what sealed their fates.

Pietro decided that he wanted to see what Bruno had told him earlier in the day about the Pelliccia farm. He took the long way home because it went by the Pelliccia farm. As he made his way to the farm he noticed that there was activity at the main house but that the land hadn't been touched in some time. Pietro decided to ride down to the main house to go see Anthony, Gilda, and, of course, Anthony's mother. As he approached the house, he started to see what was going on. His first instincts were to turn around and ride like the wind but that would have raised suspicions. It was Francisco and some Germans he had never seen before going through the main house.

There were two trucks parked next to the main entrance. One was being filled with items from the house and the other looked like another family's items waiting to be unloaded. There was a family that Pietro didn't recognized standing next to the truck. By the way they were dressed Pietro knew they were farmers, but not Italian farmers, more likely German farmers. There were about five to six family members moving furniture and suitcases off the second truck. Pietro couldn't help but notice that in-between the main house and the barn there was a clearing of land that was usually filled with a vegetable garden that Gilda worked. Instead of the usual mounds of divided dirt for the different crops, it looked like something or someone had been buried in this area because the whole section was flat and just recently filled. Francisco was overlooking the operation from his car when he turned around to see Pietro ride up on his bike and looking in the direction of the garden.

"What can I do for you, Mr. Zucchet?" asked Francisco.

"Oh nothing I was just stopping by to talk with Mr. Pelliccia about farming and what he was going to do this season," replied Pietro.

Francisco's facial expression turned from pleasant to evil.

"The Pelliccia family no longer operates this farm. It has been taken over by the state and has new farmers that will be utilizing this land for the good of the government," replied Francisco. Pietro knew what this meant and needed to be careful about how he responded to this news.

"Well let me congratulate the new farmers of this land and be on my way," replied Pietro.

"They are busy today, Mr. Zucchet. Come by another day to welcome the new family," responded Francisco.

"Very well. Have a nice day, Francisco, and thank you for the seed. It was very generous of the state to provide such a superior seed for us to grow." Francisco looked at Pietro with a smile and returned to his task of moving the new family into the main house.

Pietro turned his bike around and started his long ride home. As he turned right heading onto the main road, he looked back at the farm and old garden section shaking his head. As soon as he was far enough from the view of Francisco, Pietro rode his bike as fast as his legs would let him. During the ride home, Pietro kept thinking to himself, *Could I have caused whatever evil happened to the Pelliccia family?* He started to feel guilty about what had happened to the deserters and the Pelliccia family, but there was no way he was going to jeopardize his family for the sake of others. Pietro trusted nobody but his family. This he had learned from the first war and his father.

***

After he arrived at home, he was exiting the barn after storing the bike when Bruno, who was still watching the house for more deserters, met him.

"So, did you see any other deserters running through the fields or the roads since I left?" asked Pietro.

"No, there were no other deserters or visitors while you were gone. What is the matter, Dad, you look really sad and confused," responded Bruno. Pietro did not stop walking towards the main house and made a gesture for Bruno to follow.

"I have some news and I want to tell everyone at the same time. Where are your mother and sister?" Bruno was following his father back to the house still carrying the shotgun and ammo belt around his shoulder.

"They are both in the house," responded Bruno.

"Good, you are not going to believe what I saw and heard today," replied Pietro.

As Pietro walked into the kitchen from the back door, he saw Anna and Catherina sitting at the table getting dinner ready. Anna looked at her husband and knew right away something was wrong. Pietro grabbed the bottle of wine that was opened from the previous evening and poured himself some wine before sitting down in the kitchen. Bruno stood next to the kitchen sink waiting for his father to catch his breath before he started to tell everyone about the deserters and the Pelliccia family. After telling what had happened on such a troubling day, all he could do was to stare at his poor wife and daughter as they hugged each other and cried for the unfortunate farmers.

"What are we going to do if we have a bad crop, because it does happen?" Anna asked.

"We will do everything we can not to have a bad crop. I believe there was more to the story than just a bad crop; Anthony was too close to the Fascist movement. If you can't deliver on certain promises then they can easily turn on you if things don't work out. We have to maintain our space from this new government but yet deliver our goods as expected with the ultimate goal of surviving this period."

"I will start to get the fields ready starting tomorrow," Bruno said.

Pietro nodded with approval and added, "That is a good thing and next week I will be going into town to see what happens to the deserters. I need to know what they are planning to do because there will be more to come as the war continues."

***

As Gino approached the farm, he could see the light in the kitchen. He didn't want to scare anybody so he decided to

head to Bruno's place, which was in the back of the farmhouse.
Catherina had mentioned in one of her letters that he was living
there now to make more room in the house for Catherina and
the baby. As he made his way to the door of Bruno's room, he
stopped just before he knocked to hear if anybody was up inside
the room or if there was any movement from inside the room.
Gino knew this farm like the back of his hand from all the time he
spent there with Chester. Gino took a deep breath and knocked
on the door ever so gently.

"Bruno, this is Gino. Are you here?" whispered Gino. Gino
could hear something from the inside of the room and it sounded
like someone was getting out of the bed and putting on their
shoes.

"Gino?" Bruno said.

"Yes, it is me," answered Gino.

"Oh my god, hold on give me a minute." Bruno opened the
door and shined the gas lantern that he had lit in the direction
of Gino. "Oh my god, it is you!" He immediately gave him a hug
and they both started to laugh together.

"It's good to see you again, Bruno. Are Catherina and Maria
in the main house?"

"Oh, yes, and it looks like she is trying to feed Maria again.
She doesn't like to sleep too much so your wife has to stay up
late. Let's go see them."

Catherina was standing at the kitchen sink finishing cleaning
the dishes that she used to feed Maria. Maria was sitting in her
high chair that Pietro made out of wood watching her mother
at the sink. Catherina heard the door in the back of the kitchen
open up and continued to clean the dishes.

"Bruno, is that you?"

Bruno was the first to enter the kitchen. "Yes, it's me, and I
couldn't sleep, so I saw the light on."

Gino followed Bruno into the kitchen glancing in the
direction of his daughter to the left of the kitchen. He was
overjoyed with what he saw. Gino immediately went straight to
Catherina. Catherina was just about finished with cleaning the
sink when she turned around to see what her brother was doing.
Gino was just standing about two feet from Catherina when she
stopped her turn and gasped at the sight of her husband who

she had not seen for so long. She immediately went to him and started to cry with joy as she wrapped her arms around him.

Gino was sitting at the kitchen table with Catherina near his side when they told them the news about his father passing away. Pietro, Anna, and Bruno were all at the table when Gino received the news. He was so upset that he couldn't even talk for about ten minutes. What he realized at that moment was that he hated the Germans and wanted out of the army. The anger in him was very strong and deep and would last for the rest of his life. There was no good reason to keep playing this game that Mussolini was pushing on the Italian Royal Army. Gino was going to find a way to get out of the army and avenge the death of his father.

Catherina made Gino promise not to desert because they all knew that Fascist supporters would come to the farm and look for him. There were rumors that deserter families were the first to suffer.

After Gino explained how he arrived at the farm, Pietro looked at him with a big smile that would be given to his own sons.

"What needs to happen tomorrow is that Bruno will go with you to the train station in Pordenone. He will make sure that you get back on the train to Rome without anybody seeing you. The last thing we need is to have someone recognize you and turn you into Francisco's gang of thugs. In the future, you need to let us know when you are coming and we can make preparations for your arrival."

Gino agreed to let them know ahead of time when he was coming to visit but he wouldn't know the next time he could make it until he figures out what he would be doing in Rome.

"It's time we all go to bed so Gino and Catherina can spend some time by themselves," remarked Pietro. Anna walked over to Gino and Catherina and kissed them both as she made her way to their bedroom. Bruno excused himself as he exited to his room in the back of the main house. Catherina picked up Maria and led Gino to the bedroom that would be their sanctuary for the unforeseeable future.

Chapter 8

Auction House

IN LATE SUMMER 1941, the Axis controlled most of Europe, with the exception of some neutral countries, and Germany shifted its attention from England and invaded Russia with the help of Italy. Mussolini sent troops there to support Hitler's efforts and at the same time established the Italian 8th Army. There were still Italian troops in Africa, Albania, and Greece; Italy had surrender what was left of its army in Ethiopia. The country was starting to question what Mussolini was doing and if Germany was really the ally or the enemy. Stories of German atrocities, systematic euthanasia of the mentally ill and handicapped, and the elimination of the Jews were starting to become more of a reality to the people of Italy rather than just rumors. None of these actions sat well in a country that was mostly Roman Catholic.

Pietro was patiently waiting for the auction house to open its gates so he could bring in his crops with his horse and carriage. This was his fourth and last trip to the auction house; he so wanted a tractor but it would have to wait until after this war. With this last load Pietro made his crop goal, and Gregory again made his goal with some help from Pietro. The weather was very pleasant, which made the ride out to Cimpello less of a burden on Pietro and his last remaining horse.

Bruno usually came with him, but Pietro didn't want him to be exposed to the likes of Francisco and the other Fascist goons. Bruno would load the cart before his father left the farm, which meant that Pietro would have to unload at the auction house. He usually would get another person to help him unload after the crop was inspected and weighed. As Pietro was waiting for the gates to open, he was thinking about this year's crops and what had happened over the summer. Francisco and his goons didn't come out like he thought they would have back in the spring, although Pietro saw them driving by the farm many times. It was during these times that everyone at the farm practiced what they would do if the Italian Fascists or Germans stopped to search the farm.

The silk factory was turning out more uniforms for the soldiers, which meant they needed more workers, so Anna and Catherina were able to get some extra work while the children were in school. Bruno was the same but seemed to be stronger on the hotter days than the colder ones. The railroad would be calling for workers soon, so he would be gone most of the winter until the spring. Gino was able to visit two more times, but both again for only one day, which meant he needed to get back to Rome without being detected.

Pietro finally received a letter from Chester who was now somewhere in Egypt fighting. His unit was moved out of Ethiopia before the Italians surrendered. The letter made Anna very happy that he was alive, but she was still very concerned about him, which always made her very sad.

Pietro could finally see some movement on the other side of the gates. Since they put the walls up a couple of years ago, you couldn't see inside anymore. As the gates opened up, Pietro delivered his crops for the last time that year. Fascist supporters and the occasional German soldier had replaced almost all the locals that worked at the auction house. Today was no different, except Pietro could see that Francisco's car was parked near the office building of the auction house. He had some Germans with him doing some type of inspections. As Pietro made his way to the weight and inspection station, he moved his hat down so he wouldn't be recognized. The inspector was looking over the crops on the cart.

"Name of the farm?"

"The Zucchet farm. This is the fourth and last load," replied Pietro.

The inspector wrote something down and instructed Pietro to the unloading area. After unloading all of the corn, Pietro made his way back to the weigh station. The inspector went towards the office building.

"Hey, where are you going? Just take my weight so I can get going," yelled Pietro. The inspector just kept walking towards the office. As Pietro waited for the inspector to return, he couldn't help but feel that something wasn't right. After about ten minutes the door opened and out came Major Klein, Francisco, and the inspector. Pietro smiled, trying to look relaxed. He didn't know what they wanted, but he would be pleasant to them, knowing how cruel they could be to the farmers.

"Mr. Zucchet, congratulations on making your goal this year," remarked Major Klein. All three were smiling.

"Thank you, Major, it is good to see you again," answered Pietro in German.

"So how is the family doing?" asked Major Klein.

"They are doing fine, Major, thank you for asking," answered Pietro. "I have something for you, Major," Pietro said.

"For me? What could you have for me?" remarked the major. Pietro reached below his knees and into a wooden box that carried spare cart parts and tools. He pulled out a small potato sack and handed it to Major Klein.

"What is this, Mr. Zucchet?" asked Major Klein. Francisco was trying to see what was in the bag but was blocked by the major's broad shoulders.

"It is the hazelnuts you requested during the spring, Major," answered Pietro. "I would give them another couple of weeks to dry out, but then they should be good to eat." The major looked inside of the bag and then he turned to Francisco with a big smile.

"You remembered the hazelnuts, Mr. Zucchet. That's very nice of you."

"No problem, Major," answered Pietro. What Major Klein didn't know is that Anna always put a bag of hazelnuts in the cart for Pietro to eat during his trips to the Cimpello. Pietro enjoyed the nuts with a glass of wine and he usually shared them with some friends.

The major handed the bag to Francisco and started looking at the cart and horse. "So how long have you had this cart and horse?" Major Klein asked.

"Well I would say about ten years; it is very reliable. The horse is about the same age."

The major nodded while he was inspecting the cart and looking at the horse's legs. "It is a very nice horse, Mr. Zucchet. Do you use it to plow as well?"

"Yes, and other choirs around the farm as well," answered Pietro.

The crop inspector wrote down some numbers on a receipt and handed it to Pietro and then patiently waited for the major to tell him he could go on his way. The receipt was the most important paper that Pietro would hold all year. He would take it to the bank and get paid for all his hard work. The money would have to last until the next planting season.

Major Klein walked over to Francisco and put his arm around his shoulder as he guided him towards the office, talking to him about other issues that concerned the Germans. The inspector gave Pietro a wave, signaling he could leave.

Pietro handed his four receipts to the bank clerk; most farmers didn't really know the going prices until this point. As Pietro waited, he decided to look around the bank to see if knew anyone. He was shocked that he didn't recognize a single person. *The Fascists have totally taken over the whole banking industry*, he thought. The clerk handed him his deposit slip, which included all of the expenses that the government took out. Pietro looked over the deposit slip and couldn't believe that he made about 25 percent less than he did the previous year, even though he delivered more crops. He moved over to the side to inspect the deposit slip and noticed that the government had taken out some money for the extra seed he had thought was free and it imposed a tax. Pietro had been a farmer his whole life and never saw this before, so went back to the clerk.

"Excuse me, but what is the Horticulture Science Advisor tax?"

"That is the new tax for Major Klein's advance horticulture

education and advice to all the farmers on how to better produce crops and livestock."

Pietro knew that he couldn't fight this new tax without some type of pain coming down on his farm, so he thanked the clerk and left the bank.

***

Pietro told Anna the bad news about the money. They would have to really tighten their belts. The good news was that all of their hidden pots were full of food and should last them until the spring. He was also able to barter more sausage and cheeses with the extra corn that he grew on his extra parcel of land. Anna hung most of the sausage in the attic behind a false wall that Bruno had made the previous year. They would always leave some sausage and cheese in the kitchen in case the farm was raided, and at least there was something that could be taken by the Germans or Fascist supporters. Pietro worried something was amiss because Major Klein or Francisco had not visited the farm in a long time. *They may be planning a big raid,* he thought.

Pietro and Bruno were sitting in their normal places out front having a smoke waiting for Anna to bring them their afternoon coffee.

"When are we going to turn the soil and prep the fields?" asked Bruno.

"It will probably be the next time it rains. I think next week it will rain, so you need to make sure all the equipment is good to go," replied Pietro.

Bruno always wondered how his father could predict the weather. He was very good at it but he did get it wrong some of the time.

Anna came out and served her husband and son coffee. She looked down the road towards town.

"Is that dust coming from the road?" asked Anna. Before Pietro could say anything both Anna and Bruno were already heading into the house. Bruno knew that he was supposed to help Anna get the children in their positions and then go to his room in the back of the farm. Anna had already called out to Catherina to gather up the children so they could take their positions on the steps. Bruno was heading upstairs to make sure his grandmother was awake. Valerie, Valasco, and Maria were already in their positions. Bruno went to his room on the backside of the farmhouse.

Pietro watched the smoke turn into dust as the cars and trucks rolled towards his farm. He could see Major Klein's car leading the way and behind his car was a troop transport truck. As they made their way down the main road, Anna yelled out to Pietro that they were all ready for the visitors. *This could be another rehearsal*, thought Pietro, but this time he felt that they were going to make a left onto his farm.

Pietro put his best smile on and started to wave at Major Klein's car, which started to slow and make the left into his rocky driveway. Pietro stopped waving and put his hands into his pockets, this was the signal to Anna that they were getting visitors. Catherina immediately went into the kitchen to get refreshments ready, but she would wait until her father made the request for her to come out.

Major Klein's car came to a stop near the front door of the main house and Francisco was sitting next to him. The troop transport stopped just behind the car and Pietro could see that there were four German soldiers getting out of the back. Pietro took his hands out of his pockets and put his right hand behind his back with his ring finger extended out. Anna saw the signal to bring out the refreshments and gestured Catherina to make her way out to the driveway with the tray of goods.

"So, what brings you all the way out here, Major Klein?" asked Pietro in German. Major Klein made a hand gesture for them to sit down next to each other on the front porch. They both sat.

"Mr. Zucchet, you had a great growing season, in fact, it was the best in the region. I came here to congratulate you on your success." Just as the major was talking out came Catherina with the refreshments.

"Would you like something to drink or eat, Major?" asked Pietro. The major looked at the refreshments and declined, but Francisco who had made his way to the front of the car gestured Catherina over so he could take some wine and fruit. Pietro noticed that two of the soldiers were going into the house, while one was going to the hazelnut trees, and the last soldier was headed towards the barn.

"Mr. Zucchet, I wanted to thank you for the nuts you gave me and would like to take some more, if that is alright with you?"

"Take as many as you would like, Major," replied Pietro.

Inside the house, the soldiers searched, moving furniture, baskets, and anything that wasn't nailed down. When they reached the second floor they even checked under the mattress of Pietro's mother's bed, which required that his mother be removed. This was a large task for Anna to get his mother out of the way, but she did as she was requested for fear of repercussions. The third floor was the attic and they quickly looked around and took the couple of meat and cheeses that Pietro purposely left. As the soldiers made their way back to the first floor, they passed the three children sitting on the steps, none the wiser of what was hidden under their young bodies and the steps. Each step had a removable top that covered the perfect hiding place for the family's coin, food, and other needed valuables. The last place the soldiers always go to on their way out was the kitchen. They never leave the house without taking something from the kitchen and today would not be any different. All the wine, bread, cheese, and vegetables were confiscated, with nothing left for the family except some scraps. Anna was upset and was asking them to leave some food, but the soldiers ignored her comments because they did not speak the language and didn't really care about what she was saying. As the soldiers made their way out of the house carrying their stolen goods, Francisco stopped talking to Catherina. As the two soldiers made their way to the back of the troop transport, they dropped off all the goods into Major Klein's car. Francisco looked to see what the soldiers had taken.

Francisco ignored Catherina, walking past her as if she was invisible. As Francisco approached the main house, two soldiers were bringing Bruno by force to the cars. He wasn't resisting, but he also wasn't coming willingly. Pietro tried to defuse the situation.

"Major Klein, you remember my son Bruno. He helps me on the farm during the planting season and then works for the state during the winter on the railroad station."

"Yes, I remember him. What was he doing in the back of the farmhouse?"

"That is where his bedroom is located, Major. He doesn't sleep in the main house because we don't have the room," replied Pietro.

The soldiers approached Major Klein and one of them handed him a piece of paper with a list written on it.

"How many horses do they have?"

"Just one," Pietro replied. "The one you saw when I delivered the crops to town."

As the Major looked over the list one more time, Pietro noticed that it was an inventory of what was in the barn. The soldiers even counted the chickens. The major finished his wine, handed the list to Francisco, and then asked Pietro, "How do you think this planting season will be compared to last year, Mr. Zucchet? "

"Well, Major, that depends on the weather. If the winter is not so bad then we will have a good planting season. If the weather is very cold and we don't get the rains, then it will be a tough planting season. We are at the mercy of Mother Nature I am afraid."

"Hmm, I see. You will get your supply of seed in the spring as usual and don't forget the goal we sent for your farm," replied the major.

"Yes, Major," replied Pietro.

Both of the vehicles worked their way out of the driveway. Pietro looked at Bruno.

"Start the fire and let the other farmers know that the Germans are coming."

Bruno reached into his pocket for matches and as soon as they were out of sight, he lit the patch of dried grass in the field that was already set up for the signal.

Chapter 9

LOOKING FOR JEWS

THE WINTER OF 1941-42 was the coldest European winter of the 20th century. The temperature was much below normal from the beginning of January until the end of March. It was also during this period Europe saw a noticeable shift in the dominance of the Axis Powers. The war in Russia was not going as planned due to Germany's and Italy's lack of proper clothing. Their equipment also malfunctioned due to the snow and extreme cold. The inadequate clothing was due to the German and Italian High Command being convinced that the war would end before the arrival of winter.

Pietro was sitting in his kitchen drinking a glass a wine and thinking to himself, *This time of year I should be outside but it is too cold.* Anna was doing the dishes from dinner and they were alone for the first time in a while.

"Anna, we have been farming our whole lives. Do you remember a winter as cold as this one?" asked Pietro.

"No, Pietro, this is the coldest one so far and it couldn't have come at a worse time."

Anna and Pietro knew that they had just about used up all of their hidden resources, but they still had plenty of coin left. He knew he couldn't use the coin locally because Francisco would find out. So, he usually sent Bruno out to the surrounding towns for supplies. But Bruno had been gone since November working the railroad job, and Catharine was working at the silk factory making uniforms at night. Anna was busy as well during the day taking care of Maria and the normal farm choirs. So Pietro would go in the next couple of days for the needed supplies. The horse needed some exercise, so the trip would be good. Besides, he could find out what was really going on in the war. Pietro had heard that America had joined the war and that Russians were winning against the Germans and Italians.

"I will leave this weekend to go get supplies and be back before Monday," Pietro told his wife. Anna finished her last dish and turned around while drying her hands with a dish towel.

"Pietro, remember what Gino said when he was home? It isn't safe anymore in Rome. The violence was quickly spreading up north and that we should stay on the farm."

"Then I will bring Gregory with me, he will need supplies as well. We cannot just stay here and hope that the weather gets better as we starve. We cannot rely on Bruno or Gino. They both have bigger problems than worrying about this farm, especially Gino. If he gets caught coming up here he will be charged with desertion. He needs to stay in Rome until this war is over with or he is going to cause this family certain hardships that we don't need."

As Pietro stopped talking his thoughts wandered to Chester. They hadn't heard from him in so many months that they were worried that something horrible had happened. Just as he was thinking about his eldest son airplanes flew overhead. Since last spring there was an increase in the amount of planes flying over their farmland. During the daytime, Pietro could see that most of the planes were German and Italian, but there were some he didn't recognize. The planes had changed so much since the first war. They were much faster and louder.

The next morning Anna walked out to the barn to see what Pietro was doing so early in the morning. There he was getting the wagon and horse ready for his journey to the outside towns.

"Gregory is coming with me and we are leaving first thing in the morning. We should only be gone a couple of days at the most. Are you going to be okay while I am gone?"

"We will be fine. I will go see Marina to make sure she has everything she needs and if they want to stay here while you are gone," replied Anna.

"They are coming over tonight after it gets dark, and so are John and Mary Mazon. Gregory and I think it is safe to start having the meetings again with the few families that we trust; we all have been through so much together. John will be checking on everyone while we are gone."

Anna was a bit surprised about this news but trusted her husband. She would start to get things ready for the meeting that evening, but they didn't have all the refreshments that they had in the past—nobody did.

They were down to just three families, but Pietro didn't want to try and invite any new ones for fear of what happened with the Pelliccias. The new family working the Pelliccia farm was from Germany and everyone stayed clear of them for fear of what happened to the previous owners. Gregory and John were sitting near the horse talking with one another when Pietro walked up to them with Maria in his arms. Anna walked over to him gave him a glass of wine and took Maria away so the men could talk without any disruptions.

"So, how is everyone doing this evening?" asked Pietro. Gregory and John both smiled.

"Can you make the weather better, because I am about done with this winter, my friend," replied John. All three men started to laugh but they all knew it was a serious situation and one that the Germans wouldn't be too happy with when they don't see the right results. With the exception of Pietro, both of the other farmers barely made their crop quota.

"So tomorrow we will go to Pordenone and Azzano-Decimo for some supplies, my friend?" asked Pietro.

"Do both of you know what you need? If not, get the list ready for tomorrow. John, give your list to me or Gregory and we will take care of your needs," replied Pietro.

"Of course, you know the rule. If you see something that you or your wives would want and it is not on the list, get us some," said John. Both Gregory and Pietro started to laugh.

Anna and the other wives stopped playing with Maria to look at their husbands laughing and drinking wine. Anna couldn't remember the last time she saw her husband laugh that loud; it was a welcome site. Just as Anna was feeling a little relief in the air, a constant reminder of the war made its way past their farm. Everyone heard the rumble of planes, so they turned down the lanterns. They didn't know who was in the air, but they didn't want any bombs or sudden visitors. After a few moments, the planes roared away and the lights were turned back up. The evening came to a close with everyone going their separate way. In the darkness, Anna and Pietro cleaned up the barn as best as they could before heading to the main house for some well-deserved rest.

* * *

The next morning, Anna was still in bed when she reached for her beloved husband. The other side of the bed was empty, which meant that he was getting ready for his trip. She opened her eyes to see that the sun was just coming out and that the slightest bird noises could be heard. Anna was trying to get moving but knew she had some time because she hadn't even heard the noise from the horse and carriage, both of which usually woke up the whole house. As she lay in bed, she started to stretch her aching body when she heard people talking. There were men talking and at first she thought it was Pietro and Gregory speaking to one another, but then she heard German. She grabbed her nightgown and made her way to the kitchen to see who was outside talking. As she looked out the window she could see a German car and truck had pulled up in the stone driveway. She must have been having a really good sleep to not hear them pull up in the driveway. There was a German officer talking to Pietro, but she couldn't make out what they were saying. The officer was showing Pietro some photos, but she couldn't make out what they were talking about because they were just past the water pump. *Pietro must have been getting some water for the horse when they pulled up*, thought Anna.

As she looked around, something caught her eye to the right of where Pietro and the German officer were talking. It was Gregory hiding behind one of the haystacks. He must have been walking to the farm and saw the Germans talking to Pietro. Gregory saw Anna and waved at her like nothing was happening, but Anna just smiled at him because she was afraid that someone would see her. She was right because as she shifted her eyes back to Pietro the German officer was looking in her direction. Without hesitation she gently waved at him and raised a coffee cup as a giving gesture for a morning beverage. Pietro smiled at his wife giving her a hand movement to start the morning coffee for their guest.

"So is that your wife in the window, Mr. Zucchet?" asked the officer.

"Yes it is, and she is making us coffee, Lieutenant," replied Pietro.

"Do you think she knows the whereabouts of these Jewish families on this list of photos that I have shown you?" he asked Pietro.

"Lieutenant, my wife stays home and doesn't venture out very often. I highly doubt that she knows anybody unless they go to our church or they are a farmer within an hour of here. All the folks you showed me on this list I have never encountered or know of, with the exception of a few shop owners in Pordenone," Pietro answered.

"Well then, we are done here. If you do encounter any Jews you will report it to the local Fascists center in Cimpello."

Pietro nodded as the lieutenant put the photos and lists in his briefcase. The lieutenant walked to his waiting car, waving his hand at the truck driver to pull out. Anna could see Pietro wave Gregory towards him as the vehicles were out of sight. After about ten minutes, Anna noticed Gregory heading towards home while Pietro made his way back into the main house. He walked into the kitchen, making his way towards the kitchen table to sit down.

"What was all that about, Pietro?"

"They were looking for Jews. I told them that we didn't know any Jews and we hadn't seen any come this way. We will have to wait until tomorrow before we leave because I told them I was just out doing my morning chores and don't want to raise any suspicions. They might think that we would warn any Jews that we knew. It's best to stay home today."

***

The next morning Pietro opened the door leading to the barn, and the cold hit him so fast that it took his breath away. Gregory was standing next to the barn waiting for his life-long friend.

"Gregory, aren't you cold, my friend?" asked Pietro.

"I just got here, but yes, I am very cold, so open the door old man," replied Gregory.

They both started to laugh because Pietro was about two months older than Gregory, which was always a joke between them. Pietro quickly gave Gregory a bucket so he could get some water for the horse. Pietro started to get all the gear ready for hooking the horse up when he noticed the bikes he and Gregory could use to travel on and get to their destination faster than the horse and wagon. As Gregory walked into the barn, he saw Pietro looking at the bikes with the wagon gear hanging in between his arms.

"So which is it, Pietro, bikes or horse and wagon?" asked Gregory.

"We are going to take the wagon and one bike because we need to feed three families, so we will use both types of transportation," replied Pietro. Gregory grabbed Bruno's bike and loaded it onto the wagon.

The two men rolled out. Anna waved goodbye from the front porch and handed her husband a bag with food.

"See you in a couple of days," Pietro said. He handed the bag to Gregory who placed it beside a box full of other items to be used as barter. Pietro couldn't remember how many times the hazelnuts had come in handy, but he would keep them in case they were needed in a tight situation.

The two men rode by barren fields awaiting planting. After a couple of hours of traveling, Pietro could see that they were approaching Pordenone. He noticed that the usual hustle and bustle of a major city was missing. It was early midday, which usually meant more people walking or riding their bikes or horses around getting their daily chores done. But not today, the road leading to Pordenone was empty. It was just he and Gregory riding their wagon into town.

They were still about five minutes from the beginning of the town when Pietro noticed two freshly covered mounds of dirt on both sides of the road. As they approached, something caught his eye, so he pulled back on the reigns stopping the horse.

"What did you stop for?" asked Gregory.

"Here, hold the reigns," replied Pietro.

Pietro jumped off the wagon and walked very slowly towards the dirt, looking around to make sure nobody was watching him. When he got close enough he quickly bent down to pick up the cloth that caught his eye. He quickly got back on the wagon, grabbing the reigns from Gregory. Just as he was reaching for the newly collected piece of cloth from his jacket pocket, he noticed vehicles coming his way at a very fast rate. Pietro quickly shifted his attention to the road, motioning the horse to come right off the road to make room for the oncoming vehicle. As they got closer, he noticed it was the same cars that visited his farm yesterday. The German lieutenant was sitting in the front looking in his direction; Pietro raised his hand and made a waving gestured towards him. Pietro noticed that the lieutenant was not looking very pleased, but he could tell that he recognized him as they rolled past.

"Wasn't that the same group of soldiers that stopped at your place yesterday?" asked Gregory.

"Yes, it is, and don't look back! They will think we are hiding something," Pietro said. They both continued to look forward until they couldn't hear the vehicles. Pietro reached down so as to look like he was checking on the brake of the wagon. He could see that they were out of sight so he grabbed the piece of the cloth from his pocket. It was a yellow, very dirty, and looked like it was crumpled up in a ball. As he held the reigns in one hand he opened the yellow cloth to reveal a yellow star with the word *JUDE* written in the middle. Pietro turned the cloth over and saw blood on the other side. *The Germans must have been looking for Jews*, Pietro thought. *The yellow armband was probably from someone they captured or killed*. Pietro wondered what the Jews did to be hunted like they were animals.

***

Pietro could finally see some people walking around the city, but still it was nothing compared to what he was use to hundreds of times he made this journey. They made their way to the market area, which usually drew lots of people and goods. As they rode the wagon down the roads, they both noticed that many of the usual shops were closed. Jews had owned the shops.

"I guess all the rumors about the Jews were true," Gregory said. Pietro just nodded in agreement.

"Gregory, grab the bike and go take a look around the city for supplies while I feed and water the horse," Pietro said. Gregory grabbed the bike off the wagon, jumped on it, and headed towards an uncertain search.

Pietro was just about finished feeding the horse when he saw the Germans coming his way. It was just a small group of soldiers. Pietro put on his smile as they stopped in front of him.

"What are you doing here in Pordenone, Farmer?" asked the German sergeant.

"Just looking for supplies, Sergeant. This has been a rough winter and my family is very hungry," replied Pietro. He noticed that they all smelled like they came out of a bar.

"You haven't seen some other German soldiers have you?"

"Yes, there were two vehicles leaving the town as I was coming into Pordenone." Pietro was pointing in the direction of the road leaving town.

The sergeant tapped the driver on the shoulder and told him to go down the direction of the road leaving Pordenone. As they drove out of Pordenone, Pietro's attention turned to the bike approaching him.

"Why is it that every time I leave you alone, the Germans stop to talk to you?" said Gregory with a grin. Pietro laughed.

"What did you find out?" asked Pietro.

"Well it is what we thought. Some of the stores owned by Jews have closed, but there are still some places opened and controlled by the Fascists. I think we need to stay clear of those stores. The market is open and just down the road, but it isn't like it was a couple of years ago," Gregory continued.

"I agree with you about the stores. Let's get going before the damn Germans come back," replied Pietro.

They were looking to barter for flour, olive oil, sausage, cheese, wine, and fabric. Pietro had coin with him but didn't want to use it unless he needed too. He had eggs, hazelnuts, milk, and some seed to trade. As they walked the market, he could tell that this was a good idea. There weren't too many beggars and most of the carts were still full of items to buy or barter. After about an hour, Pietro and Gregory were done and already having some wine. All of the items that they needed were bought, but everything was poor quality. This worried Pietro because he knew it was only going to get worse as this war kept going. Pietro and Gregory were just past the end of the market having some lunch with their wine.

"So, do you want to continue our trip to Azzano-Decimo?" asked Gregory. Pietro was thinking about Gregory's question as he drank from the bottle of wine. Most of the items they needed they were able to get for all three families. Pietro had the largest family to feed and wanted to get more of everything to make sure his family was fed. If they left now, they could be home very late and wouldn't have to spend the night anywhere.

"Part of me wants to keep going to the next town, but it is getting too dangerous to travel. We should probably just call it and head back to the farms before someone decides to make us a target," Pietro said. Gregory nodded in agreement as they both started to load up the wagon for their trip home.

***

Catherine was sitting in the kitchen with Anna catching up on some sewing and other household chores. It was late in the evening and they both were very tired of watching kids and working. They both enjoyed the peace while working under the only electric light on the farm. As the light flickered as usual, they both heard the familiar sound of the horse and carriage pulling up.

"Stay here. I am going outside to see who is here," said Anna. She got up and grabbed a lantern on her way out to the front of the house. As she opened the main door to the gravel road outside, she noticed the horse right away.

"Did you have any problems?" asked Anna. Pietro was already off the wagon and getting the supplies off the wagon when he smiled at his wife.

"Not really, but every time we looked around we saw Germans, so we just went to Pordenone and came back. I already dropped Gregory off and gave Johnny his supplies."

Anna helped Pietro unload all the supplies from the wagon.

Catherine came out as soon as she knew it was her father and helped her mother hide all the supplies in the stairs, attic, and near the hazelnut trees. Pietro took the horse and carriage to the barn. He moved the horse to his resting place and put down some well-deserved hay for him to eat. As he made his way back to the main house, he looked up as the planes flew over his small farm.

"This war is just getting started," said Pietro.

Chapter 10

TRAIN STATION

THE DOOR TO THE empty train station opened and Francisco made his way towards the track. The whole station had been cleared of all citizens to limit the exposure of what was getting ready to happen. He was actually smiling for the first time in a while because he wasn't wearing his coat. Warmer weather had finally arrived. He walked towards the track looking for the train that was heading to Poland and would make the stop in Pordenone to pick up all the Jews and Gypsies who had been rounded up. They were told that they were going to be sent away until the war was over with and then they would return to continue their lives in Italy.

Francisco walked towards the make-shift holding area to check on his passengers. As he approached he could see one of his subordinates waiting for his arrival.

"Are we ready to the load these Jews and Gypsies on the next train?" asked Francisco.

The guard saluted. "Yes, we are, sir."

Francisco looked around the area and made one last look at his paperwork.

"They all have a lot of luggage, sir. How are we going to fit all of it on the train?" asked the guard.

"When the train arrives, tell them to only take one suitcase per family. Then tell them that there will be another train after this one that will take the rest of their luggage and meet them at their final destination."

Just as Francisco got done talking to the guard, he could hear the four o'clock train make its way towards the station.

***

Catherina was getting ready to leave from the silk factory and head home to her family. She wasn't feeling the best these days and that was probably because she was due to have her second child. She hadn't seen Gino in about three months and probably wouldn't see him until this war was over. As she got on her bike, she made her way down the road towards the road leading out of town, which went by the train station. She had heard about the Jews and Gypsies being transported. Her father had told her that they wouldn't be coming back, despite what the Germans told them.

As she made her way out of the town, she was getting hot and decided to stop to remove her winter jacket and place it in the basket in the front of her bike. She was getting close to the old train overpass, which allowed bikes and pedestrians to travel below the tracks. Catherina was removing her jacket when she heard the train noise and soldiers yelling from her left side. She had never heard soldiers yelling at the train station before and wanted to get a better view of what was happening in her town. She grabbed her bike and made her way through the tall bushes that surrounded the tracks. At about two hundred yards away, Catherina made it to a clearing to view what was occurring.

Francisco was watching as the soldiers were yelling at the Jews and Gypsies to get ready to board the train. Most were complying, but there were a few who didn't want to board without all of their possessions. There was a German officer sitting at a desk that was placed near the edge of the train tracks who was looking at the records that Francisco had given to him.

"Is this all of them, Deputy?" asked the officer. The Jews and Gypsies looked miserable, cold, and hungry.

"Yes, that is all of them in this area, Major," answered Francisco as he continued to look at the other cars full of Jews.

"Have them start to line up and come to me so I can interview them," the major said. "After I interview them my soldiers will place the men in the front empty boxcar and the women and children in the back boxcar. Let's get started. We have other Jews to pick up and Poland is a long way from here."

Catherina could see them being loaded on the boxcars. First the men and then the women and children; it was chaotic with most of the woman and children screaming for their men to join them. It didn't take very long, but Catherina couldn't help but cry for them for being deported for no reason except their religious beliefs. She wanted to leave and get back to her family, but she was scared that the Nazi guards would see her looking at what was going on and arrest her. She stood still among the bushes with her bike at the base of her feet. Before she knew it, all the Jews were loaded on the train and the guards followed them back on the train as well. She noticed that Francisco saluted the German officer.

Catherina was just about ready to make her move towards her bike when she noticed there was quite a bit of luggage and furniture being left behind by the Jews and Gypsies. She waited for them to finish before she dared to move.

Francisco ordered the guards to load up all the extra luggage and furniture onto two troop transporters. They would take all the personal possessions to the auction house for inspection and redistribution if there were of any value. Francisco got into the passenger seat of one of the transport trucks. He wanted to make sure that nothing was taken of value, plus he needed some new dresses for Betty. As they pulled away from the train station Francisco ordered the first truck to go ahead of him so he could keep an eye on it. As they made their way to the auction house, Francisco was looking into the side view mirror to make sure nothing was happening in the back of his truck. As he looked into the mirror he noticed a woman getting on her bike and riding off in the opposite direction of the convoy.

The journey only took about fifteen minutes before they entered the auction house.

"I want everything unloaded off the trucks and placed in three areas," Francisco ordered. "Put the furniture in area one after you remove all the items you find in the furniture. Place all items taken from the furniture in area three. Empty all the contents of the luggage in area three and place the empty luggage in area two."

Francisco was marking the three areas in the dirt with his boot at the same time he was giving instructions to the soldiers. The German officer that had taken the Jews and Gypsies had instructed Francisco to look for valuables, which included art, jewelry, and precious metal. Once the valuables had been collected, he would have to inventory them and make a report to his superiors. Once the inventory was completed, he instructed his soldiers to burn all the furniture and luggage.

Francisco grabbed two soldiers that were not interested in any items and instructed them to carry all the valuable items to his office that he shared with Major Klein. Francisco stood behind the soldiers to ensure they carried the items, including the three dresses that he thought Betty would like, to their final destination without making detours. Once the items were placed in the office, Francisco placed all of the valuables in a closet that he locked with a key. He grabbed the three dresses and made his way out of the office.

Catherina arrived home with a heavy heart as she thought about the deported families. As she made her way to the barn, Pietro was working on his spring equipment. The weather had turned so that he would have to move the soil before the planting season.

"What disturbs you, Catherina?" asked Pietro.

"You were right, Dad, they just loaded all the Jewish and Gypsy families in this area on trains," replied Catherina.

"How do you know that, Catherina, and where is your jacket?" asked Pietro. In her haste to leave the wooded area she lost her jacket while getting on her bike to come home.

"It must have fallen on the way home."

"No worries. Go inside and help your mother. I will go see if the jacket is still on the road."

"It is probably near the wooded area by the railroad tracks."

"Tell your mother that I will be home before supper," replied Pietro. He walked his bike to the road and headed towards town to get his daughter's coat.

***

As Francisco was walking home to his apartment, he stopped to talk with his supporters at the coffee shop across the street from the train station. Most of the talk was about how the Germans and Italians had not taken Russia yet. Francisco finished his coffee and walked towards his apartment. Just past the railroad tracks, Francisco could see someone going into the wooded area just before the station. He saw Pietro coming out holding a woman's jacket.

"So, what are you doing in the woods with a woman's jacket, Pietro?"

"Just getting something that belongs to me."

Pietro nodded politely, got on his bike with Catherina's jacket, and started his way back to his farm.

Francisco opened the door to his apartment to find Betty making dinner. He set the dresses down on the small couch that was in the living room.

"What is for dinner?" asked Francisco.

"Pasta, sausage, and wine, my lover," responded Betty. She turned around from the stove to see Francisco pouring himself a glass of wine.

"I have a surprise for you, my love. They are on the couch," said Francisco.

Betty couldn't help herself as she went to see what was in the living room. As she went past Francisco, he smiled for a moment as he looked at Betty bending over looking at the dresses. He was sipping his wine when it hit him, that the woman coming out of the wooded area earlier today at the railroad tracks was Catherina.

Chapter 11

MISSING ANIMALS

ANNA WAS GETTING DINNER ready and was looking out into the fields through the kitchen window. She could see Pietro working the fields with Bruno; it was harvesting time and the horse wasn't doing as well as he had in the past. Pietro would be very tired when he came home. Pietro had been working the horse non-stop this summer. The Germans were not going to let up on crop production. Catherine stood next to her mother watching both men struggle with the horse.

"Why doesn't he just use the cow when the horse acts up?" asked Catharine.

"Your father is afraid that the cow will get hurt and then how will we have any milk to drink and sell. I don't know who is more stubborn, the horse or your father," answered Anna.

"That is enough! Take the horse back to the barn, feed him, give him as much water as he wants, and put him in his stable. We will try again tomorrow morning," Pietro told Bruno.

"Okay, Dad, I will check to make sure that his shoes are good and that he isn't in any pain as well."

"If he doesn't start to perform we are going to have to go with the cow and you know that I hate to use that damn cow, it is so demeaning. If we don't finish this crop soon, Major Klein will be here to take this farm, and we cannot let that happen, so get that horse back to the barn."

Bruno did what he was told, but he was as tired as the horse and he wasn't getting any better. He usually spent most of his days off sleeping, only coming out to eat his mother's dinners. Working on the railroad during the winter really took the life out of him. In the past two years all Italian men who didn't serve must work the railroad. Bruno was working a lot harder fixing railroad tracks destroyed by allied bombing.

Pietro knew Bruno was sick, but didn't want to admit it, and neither did Anna. They continued to treat him as if he was completely normal with the exception of allowing him into the main house with the children. Anna and Catherina were constantly cleaning the house after Bruno for fear of spreading his sickness to other members of the family.

Pietro needed Bruno's help with the crops until Chester could come back from the war. At least Chester was safely in Germany right now, but for how long? Pietro had learned that Chester's army unit had refused to fight for Germany in Egypt. The German's needed their Italian allies and didn't want to send the wrong message to the royal family of Italy, so they decided to imprison resistors like Chester in German labor camps. Pietro knew this wasn't good for Chester, but it was better than being killed for a fight that no one would remember.

As Pietro turned towards the farm, he stopped to look at the condition of the house, barn, and the surrounding areas. The roofs of all the structures looked good, and there were no broken windows. Fences were all in good order, and overall everything looked acceptable. But something didn't seem right. Then it hit him; there were fewer chickens, goats, and sheep running around the farm. Pietro made his way to the farm and started to count all the animals and sure enough they only had half of their livestock.

Pietro entered the kitchen to find his wife sitting and mending clothes.

"Anna, I just counted all the animals and we have only about half of what we normally do this time of the season. What happened to all the animals?"

"Pietro, I have been telling you for months that every time the Germans come here they take either some chickens or some other animals, but you're always talking with the soldiers and you don't notice what is taken."

"How much coin do we have left since we took it out of the bank?" asked Pietro.

"We have about half the money left with nothing really coming in except for the crops, Bruno's income, and Catherina's job at the silk factory. We probably need to start hiding the animals or they will eventually all be taken. There are only so many farms here that still have animals to take," replied Anna.

"Damn it, do we have to hide everything?" yelled Pietro. He made his way out the back door of the kitchen heading towards the barn. As he entered the barn, Bruno was taking care of the horse and cow.

"We need to start hiding the animals before the Germans take everything from this farm," said Pietro.

"Well we could always put some of the animals in the roof of the barn and then rotate them every so often," answered Bruno. Pietro looked up in the barn and started to laugh.

"That is a great idea. We just need to put some more wood planks up there and some food but it would work," said Pietro.

"I was just kidding, Dad."

Pietro wasn't kidding. He was already counting the old wooden planks in the corner to see if they had enough.

"Give me a hand with these planks. We need to make a ladder to get up into the rafters but it has to be located so nobody can see it."

Bruno started to get the planks together for his father. Pietro was on the other side of the cow's pen looking up.

"Here is what we are going to do, Bruno. Bring me the ladder over in the corner of the barn," said Pietro, who was already removing some farm equipment that they stored in that corner. "Put the ladder right here, Bruno. With the ladder in this location we will nail some more steps leading to the rafters. We will keep the ladder in the corner and then nobody will notice the steps leading to the rafters."

Anna headed out to the barn to see what her husband was up to. She could hear the noise but her husband and son were nowhere to be seen. Then she looked up to see them nailing some boards across the rafters.

"I am afraid to ask what is going on, but I have to ask what are you two doing up there?"

"Well we are building a new home for some of our animals. You were right that I wasn't paying attention to what was going on with our animals, so now we are going to hide at least half of them," replied Pietro.

"How did you two get up there?" she asked.

"Look past the cow and you will see how we got up here," replied Pietro. She walked around the cow then saw the ladder with additional steps attached using rope that led up to the rafter area. "When we want to get up here, you pull on that rope you see on the right. The extension ladder will roll down to the top of the ladder. We will keep the ladder out of the barn so nobody gets any ideas about getting up here," replied Pietro with a smile from ear to ear.

"What happens if the Germans come here and notice that there are chickens up in the rafters?" asked Anna.

"We tell them that they always fly up here to get away from the rooster and that they usually get down in the evening to go back in the hen house for sleeping and eating," answered Pietro. "Hopefully they don't hear the other animals we have up here, but we can say that we have been having some troubles with stray dogs killing them so we keep them up here for safety."

***

It was almost dark when Pietro and Bruno finished with installing the floor in the barn rafters.

"Tomorrow we will get some chickens and one of the goats to see how they do up here. Take the empty feed sacks and lay them down on the floor. We also will need some hay on top of the sacks with some water and food," Pietro instructed.

"That will be fun trying to get a goat up there let alone some chickens," answered Bruno.

"You may have to tie them up so they don't kick you or scratch you. Why don't you meet me in the front of the house for some dinner, coffee, and a smoke," replied Pietro.

"Sure, just let me clean up first," answered Bruno.

Later on that week, Pietro was on top of the wagon getting his first load ready for transportation to the auction house when his son came over to give him a hand.

"Well I am glad that is over with and the horse was able to get going the last couple of days. I think it was all the time I spent in the barn the last couple of days that did it. He was lonely and just needed some attention," remarked Bruno.

"It is a horse, he has no feelings, especially that one," replied Pietro, pointing at the horse tied up at the barn. As Pietro was looking at the horse, he noticed his son looking in the distance towards the town.

"They are coming," yelled Bruno. He immediately ran towards the main house to get them ready for their visitors. Pietro looked in the distance and could see the clouds of dust headed in their direction. This wasn't the normal cloud of dust that a couple of vehicles made; this was a much larger one, which meant more soldiers and more problems. Pietro looked around the barn area before he made his way to the rocky driveway. There were just enough chickens and goats to make it look normal; the other half were already up in the rafters being quiet for the most part.

"Is everyone in their places and food tokens out for their taking?" yelled Pietro.

"We need some more time, Pietro!" yelled Anna.

Pietro rushed to the driveway entrance and pulled an old cart from the bushes that was missing a wheel. He prepositioned the smaller cart to delay the Germans. He moved it into the middle of the driveway and tipped it over so it looked as if he was working on it. Just as he grabbed a metal pry bar to start getting the lug off of the axle, he looked up to see Major Klein's sedan, which stopped to avoid hitting the cart and Pietro. There were three vehicles following the major's car. Pietro grabbed a rag from his back pocket to clean his hands as he walked around the cart to greet his guests. Francisco stepped out of the sedan.

"How can I help you, Francisco?" asked Pietro.

"Well you can start by moving that cart out of the way so we can get to your driveway, Mr. Zucchet," yelled Francisco.

"I would, Francisco, but I will need a hand getting it out of the way. I am not as strong as I used to be. Let me get the wheel back on and then can you have a couple of your friends help me get it out of the way."

"Hurry up with the wheel and we will get a couple of soldiers to help you," replied Francisco. Pietro noticed that the entourage comprised of German soldiers only. Fascist sympathizers had either been sent to the front to fight or fled in fear of the Germans.

Pietro made his way back to the cart and was looking in the direction of the main house to see if everything was ready for their unscheduled visitors. The signal was for Bruno and Anna to be standing out front, but neither was outside yet, so he needed to stall them longer. He could hear the Germans getting out of the troop transporter and heading in his direction.

"Can you get this wheel back into the axle hole so I can get the grease on it and put the pin into the axle?" As the soldiers grabbed the wheel, Pietro was getting the grease from his pre-staged rag to put on the axle before the wheel would be put on axle. The two soldiers lifted the wheel and held it in place while Pietro applied the grease with the rag. As he applied the grease, he could see Anna and Bruno exit the house from the corner of his eyes.

"Hurry up, old man!" yelled Francisco.

"I am almost done with the grease, and then the soldiers can put the wheel on the axle," answered Pietro. After a few more minutes he was done. The soldiers raised the wheel and then placed it onto the axle. Pietro then put the pin in the hole with his hammer. "Okay, the cart is ready to be lifted." Then the soldiers, Pietro, and Bruno, who just arrived, lifted the cart back on its two wheels. It was pulled to the ditch so all the vehicles could get through to the driveway, but the troop transporter stayed out on the main road. *That's odd*, thought Pietro as he made his way to the main house. Catherina was already outside with the beverages for Major Klein and Francisco.

The major got out of the car and greeted Anna and Catherina as he looked at Francisco with frustrated eyes. Francisco was noticeably nervous around the major, but more so than usual. Francisco grabbed a glass a wine from Catherina and began to sip it as he stared at her.

"Mr. Zucchet, I see that you are getting ready to make your run into town with this year's crop," Major Klein said.

"Why yes, I was about to get the first load ready to transport to town after I fixed the cart," answered Pietro.

"So I see that we have already loaded one cart. Where are the other loads?" asked the major.

"On the other side of the barn, Herr Major," answered Pietro. The major continued to sip his wine as Anna handed Pietro the Major Klein's usual prize of bagged hazelnuts. Pietro started to hand the bag of treats to the major when Francisco stopped him. Francisco took the nuts from Pietro as the major turned to see the exchange. The major smiled to see that Pietro had remembered.

"I see that you have my usual dessert treats, Mr. Zucchet. We won't be bothering you with the usual taking of the crops to the auction house this year. My men will load the grain onto the truck for transportation to the town's train station to save time."

The back gate of the truck opened and ten soldiers jumped out to load the sacks of grain. With Bruno's help they were done in about twenty minutes. Pietro stayed with the major and Francisco without saying a word. He noticed Francisco eyeing his daughter, who was obviously pregnant. After the grain was loaded, a couple of soldiers grabbed two chickens.

"Major, we didn't weight or count the crop like we have done since I was a farmer. How am I going to get paid for this crop?" asked Pietro.

"Your account has been updated at the bank based on the last two years of crops, Mr. Zucchet. This is much faster than the past, which allows us to feed our troops quicker." Pietro was at a loss for words as the caravan made its way back to the main road for their next farm. Pietro was upset.

"Did you top off our pots with this year's crops like I asked you, Bruno?" asked Pietro.

"I did it last night, just in case we had problems, but I didn't expect this to happen," answered Bruno. Anna approached and Pietro grabbed his wife's hand and kissed it.

"Bruno, give me a hand with the cart, that wheel just doesn't look right. We may have to put it back to work on it later." Pietro laughed.

"Most of the soldiers looked very nervous and afraid," Pietro told Anna. "For the first time I even noticed that Major Klein was a little shaken up. This means that the Germans are starting to feel the pain of this war for the first time. I saw this during the first war; let's just hope this lasts and that we don't feel too much pain from their defeats."

Chapter 12

LORETTA ARRIVES

IN THE FALL OF 1942, the Italian Army had about one hundred thirty thousand troops in Russia. Mussolini had scaled up the Italian effort on the Eastern Front with the 8th Italian Army. Most of the troopers were there to support the Germans and other Axis Powers countries along the Don River. In November 1942, the Soviet Union launched Operation Uranus and was able to encircle the German forces in Stalingrad and turn the tide in favor of the Soviet Union. The causalities on the Italian forces during this period were light, but that would change in a few months.

***

Anna was minding her kitchen, taking care of her morning chores and wondering what her two sons and Catherina's husband were doing in this frigid weather in the north. Chester was in Germany doing slave labor for the Germans and Bruno was off to work the railroads for another winter. He was getting sicker and weaker every time he came home before the planting season. She would take care of him during the summer and fall months, but just when he seemed to be back to full strength, winter set in and off he went to serve the Germans.

Gino was still in Rome doing his work for the city, but Catherina and her parents weren't sure why he hadn't been discharged. He had been a blessing this winter by somehow getting food, blankets, and other items to the farm. Pietro would take the extra items to town and sell them or barter. As the war in Europe continued, the flow of supplies to small towns dwindled to just about nothing.

Pietro never complained about how many people were living on the farm. "The more people we have living on the farm, the less work I have to do and the more we can plant," he would say. Anna knew he was kidding, but in a way he was right. Catherina had her second child, Loretta, and Maria was two now and moving around like she owned the farm. She was always helping out in the kitchen or going outside to spend time with her grandfather and uncle. Anna had already showed her how to plant potatoes in the ground, which helped out a lot since Anna's back wasn't as strong as it was when she was younger.

Pietro was sitting at a table right next to the bar having some wine with Greg, discussing local issues and the war. There were rumors that the Italian forces in the Soviet Union had been defeated and the causalities were severe. Rumors of the Germans killing thousands of Jews and other folks in concentration camps were also pervasive. Nobody that left this region for temporary relocation had ever come back, not even for a visit. Most of the people living in this region were spared the harsh punishments because they provided much needed food, but if they got caught doing something that the Germans or Fascists felt was detrimental to their well being they would be punished harshly.

Pietro rolled up to the farmhouse after he dropped off Greg at his farm. It was getting late but the sun was still shining. Pietro moved the cart into the barn for fear of anybody seeing what was under the burlap cover and the compartment under his seat. Anna was already making her way to the barn with Maria, Valerie, and Velasco in tow to help unload the cart. As they entered the barn, Pietro was unhooking the horse.

"So, how did your trip into town fare this time?" asked Anna.

"It went well, the market was steaming with goods this week," replied Pietro as he winked at his wife. "Where is Catharina?" asked Pietro.

"She hasn't come home from the silk factory yet," answered Anna. Pietro started to head towards his bike when Anna stopped him.

"She doesn't like it when you go check on her, Pietro, give her more time. At least wait until the sun is almost down before you go looking for her."

Not long afterward, Catharina arrived home looking sullen.

"What is wrong? Bad day at work?" asked Pietro.

Catharina turned to look at her father and replied, "No, I just saw something on the way home that was very sad. The Germans are getting very aggressive with everyone they stop."

"What did you see?" asked Pietro as he stopped what he was doing to better hear his daughter's answer.

"They are just searching everyone and taking everything they want," replied Catharina.

"I am going to Greg's house to tell him what Catharina just told me," replied Pietro. As he grabbed his bike, Maria grabbed her grandfather's hand and asked to go with him. He picked her up and rode off. About half way up Greg's driveway he dismounted the bike with Maria in his arms to avoid the rocky driveway.

Just as Pietro was making the turn towards Greg's barn he saw a motorcycle with a sidecar at the entrance. Pietro put his left hand over Maria's mouth and whispered to her to be quiet. He backed his way out so as not to be noticed by the German soldiers who were talking to Greg. Pietro quickly headed back to the bike for his escape, hoping they didn't notice them leaving. Pietro didn't even look back for fear he would be seen. It was the fastest trip back home he had ever done, even with an extra passenger.

Maria didn't even say a word the whole way home, she just sat on his lap holding on for dear life as her grandfather pedaled very quickly. Pietro made the turn into his farm and could see Anna and Catharina looking in his direction, they both knew something was wrong. Catharina grabbed Maria off his lap with a quickness that he had never seen before.

"What is going on?" asked Anna.

"There are Germans at Greg's place. Did you hide all the goods?" asked Pietro. Anna nodded her head as he passed her with his bike in tow heading towards the barn. Pietro entered the barn to see if everything looked normal and then headed back to the main house. Anna was in the house getting ready for the possible visitors when Pietro entered.

"I am going outside to have a smoke," said Pietro as he poured himself some wine. As Pietro went by the main room heading towards the front porch he noticed that Catharina was getting all the children to their positions on the steps. He went outside and sat on his normal seat to wait for their visitors.

As Pietro settled into to his normal position, his thoughts drifted to his son Bruno. It was always a lot easier dealing with the Germans when Bruno was here on the farm. Bruno knew what to say and how to act around the Germans. He learned this from watching the other workers on the railroad yard.

Pietro finished his smoke and he could see the dust of a small vehicle coming towards his farm. "Get ready, here they come!" yelled Pietro. After about a minute or two, the motorcycle made its turn into the long driveway into the farm. A German shepherd was sitting on the lap of the soldier in the sidecar. They had never brought dogs to the farm before and Pietro wondered what the dog would do when he saw the chickens. Just as the motorcycle stopped the dog saw the chickens and took off after them, the soldier in the sidecar tried to hold him back but failed. The sidecar soldier chased the dog, but Pietro knew there wasn't much he could do to prevent the demise of some of his chickens. Pietro moved his attention to the soldier on the motorcycle. He was a major of some type of intelligence branch of the army. *What's he doing here?* thought Pietro.

"Can I help you, Herr Major," Pietro said. The major finished taking off his goggles and gloves before he dismounted the bike. He reached into the side cart and pulled out a binder that had some German notation written on the front.

"Are you Mr. Pietro Zucchet, and is this your farm?" asked the German officer.

"Yes, I am Pietro and this is my farm."

Anna arrived with a plate of wine, cheese, and sausage. The major's eyes lit up. He went past Pietro towards Anna to accept their gifts of food and wine. Pietro smiled to himself and thought, *This guy is new to the area; they never eat or drink before the locals they don't know for fear of being poisoned.*

As the major drank his wine Pietro reached for another glass and joined his guest.

"So, let's talk about who lives on your farm to make sure our records match up," said the major to Pietro. The German gestured as if they should go into the house because of the cold, but Pietro never invited the Germans inside the main house. Pietro had already walked over to his bench and sat down, waiting for the major to join him. After about ten minutes, the major was satisfied that his records matched what Pietro had told him.

"So your oldest son, Chester, is in Germany right now performing duties for our country and your other son Bruno is working the railroad detail, is that correct?" asked the major.

"That is right; everyone else is living here on the farm," replied Pietro. The major was taking notes when the other soldier came around the corner with the German shepherd in tow. The dog had black and red feathers mixed with blood around its mouth and front paws, but he also had scratches on his front nose.

"So, what did the dog do to my chickens?" asked Pietro.

"Not much, since the rooster had its way with him. That is one tough rooster you have there, Mr. Zucchet. He is a little banged up but I was able to get the dog under control before he could get a good bite out of him," replied the German soldier.

"Shall I take the dog into the house to look around, Herr Major?" asked the soldier who was visibility cold and tired.

"There will be no need for that. Let's get going before it gets really cold. Thank you for your time, Mr. Zucchet."

"It was nice meeting you, Major, and stay warm on your ride back to town," replied Pietro.

"I do have one more question before I leave. Where is the father of your daughter's two young children?" asked the major.

"He is a private in the Royal Italian Army. He was badly wounded overseas and is in Rome supporting your troops that are stationed in the city," responded Pietro.

"That is very interesting. What is his name please?" asked the major.

"Private Gino Cartelli," answered Pietro. The major wrote down everything that Pietro said.

"Does he come here and visit?" asked the major.

"No, we haven't seen him in over a year or more," answered Pietro.

"Very well, thank you for your time." The major finished his wine while putting his goggles and gloves back on for the ride back to town.

Chapter 13

Bruno Arrested

THE WEATHER WARMED AND the ground was getting soft on the Zucchet farm. There was a slight wind coming down from the mountains, which was perfect to keep bugs from bothering the farmers in the fields. Most of the trees were still barren, but a few were starting to show their early season blooms.

Catherina was out in the fields with her daughters and mother. Anna was showing Maria how to plant the potatoes and Loretta was frolicking. As Catherina looked around to see her daughter being taught by the same woman who taught her how to plant potatoes over twenty years ago, she smiled and switched her attention to Loretta who was picking up old pieces of hay. From the distance she could see Pietro cleaning out the barn.

Pietro was moving the horse out of the barn so he could do his spring-cleaning, but the horse wasn't very thrilled about being moved from the comfort of the barn. Pietro finally got the horse out of the barn and moved on to the cow, but she wasn't as temperamental as the horse. Next, all the gear associated with plowing, growing, and everyday farm usage was removed. As Pietro started to sweep, he noticed that the smaller animals that were hidden in the upper level of the barn were making the place even more unbearable than normal. Even the sacks that were placed to prevent droppings were in need of replacement.

The Germans had not dropped off the seed that he had received the previous years. He smiled at the thought, knowing that the Germans had bigger issues than distribution of farm seed. Pietro continued with his spring-cleaning with a devilish smile. He knew that the Germans were starting to loss their hold on Europe, just like they did in his war. He carefully moved the ladder in place to go on top of the barn to see what kind of mess was present with the hidden animals. This wasn't going to be an easy clean up, and he would need someone to hand him some buckets of water to wash away the animal waste. As he worked his way down the ladder he looked out through the barn doors and could see the dust coming from the town. There would be no time to set up the house. Valerie and Velasco were in school and the rest of the family was in the fields planting potatoes. Pietro closed the barn doors and made his way towards the house.

Anna was watching her two grandchildren when she heard Pietro's whistle. Her and Catherina looked towards Pietro and then shifted their attention towards the area where he was pointing. Anna saw the dust and grabbed Maria by the hand while Catherina went to scoop her youngest for the run back to the house.

The German sedan lead a troop transport vehicle with eight German soldiers. Sitting beside them was Bruno, who was on his way home from another winter with the Germans. Bruno was taken from the train station in Pordenone. Nothing was said to him. All he knew was that when the train stopped the Germans were waiting for him to get off. He was escorted to the vehicle and loaded up with the other German soldiers. He had no idea what was going on, but it wasn't going to be good for the family.

As they made their way past Cimpello, Bruno knew the family would be outside doing some planting. The dirt road was extremely rough from the winter, which made the ride in the back of the transport very rocky. Bruno and the soldiers held the upper bars to keep them from being tossed around and possibly ejected from the transport. As they made their way towards the farm, Bruno could see his family out in the fields moving towards the main house. *They won't be ready for the Germans,* he thought. Suddenly, the transport jolted up into the air from a huge hole in the road. Bruno seized this opportunity by letting go of the upper bar and falling out of the transport.

The German officer in charge of the transport was cranky from chasing rebel Italians. He looked in the side mirror and saw Bruno tumble out. He ordered the driver to stop.

The delay gave Pietro and the family enough time to get to the house and take their positions. He was already in front of the main house when the car and truck pulled up. He could tell that the German officer was in no mood for beverages or pleasantries.

"Go back inside and sit next to the children," Pietro ordered Catherina, who had been standing ready to serve snacks and wine.

"Mr. Zucchet, is this your son?" asked the officer as Bruno was unloaded from the transport. He stepped down gingerly, having sprained his ankle when he fell off the truck.

"Yes it is," answered Pietro as a soldier was escorting Bruno towards him.

"Where has your son been the last few months?" asked the officer.

"He has been working for the German government fixing railroads like he has the past four years," answered Pietro as he grabbed his son's arm to help him keep his balance.

"Where is your other son, Chester?" asked the officer.

"He is in Germany supporting your country, just like I told the major who came here a few weeks ago," remarked Pietro.

"Where is Gino Cartelli?" asked the officer.

"He is in Rome working for the German military as an electrician," answered Pietro.

As Pietro was being interrogated, three soldiers entered the house and two others went to the barn.

"When was the last time you talked with Gino Cartelli?" asked the officer.

"It has been at least four months since we have seen a letter from him, and we haven't seen him in over a year," answered Pietro.

"Where is his wife?" asked the officer.

"She is inside with her children," answered Pietro.

"Mr. Zucchet, go get your daughter and bring her here." Pietro turned towards the front door, pulling Bruno with him so he could get him inside for safety.

"Your son stays here with us," ordered the officer. A soldier that had a hold of Bruno's left arm pulled him away. Pietro made his way into the house to get Catherina, who was sitting next to the children.

"Catherina, take the children to your mother and come outside so they can talk to you about Gino," said Pietro.

When Pietro went back outside, Bruno was on his knees in the middle of the driveway with his hands tied behind his back. Pietro knew this wasn't good for his son, but he was helpless.

"Herr Officer, may I ask you why you have my son in the middle of the driveway with his hands tied? Has he done something wrong?" asked Pietro.

"You are asking too many questions, Mr. Zucchet. Go sit down on your bench while we speak to your daughter." As Pietro did as he was told he looked out into the distance and could see more road dust being sent in the air, which meant they were going to have more visitors.

Catherina emerged from the house to see her brother on his knees and her father sitting on his bench. She looked at the German officer who was standing next to Bruno looking over a pad of paper.

"Mrs. Cartelli, when was the last time you heard from your husband, Gino?"

"It's been four months since we have gotten a letter from him," yelled Pietro. The German officer was getting upset with Pietro and ordered one of the soldiers to stand guard over him.

"Mr. Zucchet, you will shut up or your son will not be getting up from his current position," said the German officer who pulled out his pistol and pointed it at Bruno's head.

"Wait, please, don't shoot. I will answer your questions," Catherina pleaded. "I received a letter from my husband about four months ago, and the last time I saw him it was over a year ago. He is stationed in Rome working for the German military as an electrician." As Catherina finished talking, a sedan pulled into the stone driveway with two people inside. Pietro could see that it was Major Klein and Deputy Chief Francisco.

"What is going on here!" yelled Major Klein to the other German officer.

"This is not your matter, Herr Major. This is a Gestapo issue and we think they know where Private Gino Cartelli is located," replied the German officer. Just as the Gestapo officer finished talking the soldiers from the barn and the house both came back to the front of the house. One of the soldiers that came from the direction of the barn went to the Gestapo officer and whispered something to him. The Gestapo officer pointed the gun at Bruno's head.

"Who lives in the room in the back of the main house?"

"The person who lives in that room is on the other side of your pistol. Now put your weapon away and come here so we can talk!" yelled Major Klein. The Gestapo officer looked in the direction of Pietro and Catherina who were both nodding their heads in agreement with the Major Klein.

"If anybody moves, shoot them!" yelled the Gestapo officer as he put his weapon away and headed in the direction of Major Klein. Both officers walked towards the main road and stopped about halfway towards the main road.

"Herr Captain, do you know what you are doing to this family? Better yet, do you know what you are doing to one of our main sources of food?" asked Major Klein.

"I don't care. We are looking for a deserter," replied the captain.

"Did he tell you that he knew where the private was located?" asked Major Klein.

"No, they all say they haven't seen him in over a year, but I don't believe these scum Italian farmers," replied the captain. Major Klein looked in the direction of Pietro and Catherina before he replied to the captain's remark.

"Herr Captain, this farming community is the most productive in this region. Mr. Zucchet is the lead farmer of this area with just about every farmer in his back pocket. I have had three years of contact with him and have never had an issue with this family. If they say they haven't seen Private Cartelli, then they are telling you the truth. If you hurt anybody from this family, I guarantee this man will make sure we don't get our necessary crops this year," Major Klein said.

"Very well, Herr Major, but we will be watching them in the future just to make sure this rebel doesn't pay them a visit," replied the captain as he and the major headed towards the soldiers.

"Herr Sergeant, stand down and load everyone up, we are heading back to town," yelled the captain. Francisco was already in the sedan backing it out for the unwanted Gestapo captain and his crew to leave the farm. Major Klein walked up to the main house entrance and stood next to Pietro.

"Would you like something to drink, Major Klein?" asked Pietro.

Catherina had already gone to retrieve the beverages from the house.

"Yes, that would be nice, my throat is very dry from the dirt road and talking with the Gestapo," answered the major.

As the convoy left the farm, there was silence between the two men as Bruno got up and walked into the house for some needed first aid from his mother and sister. Pietro dared not leave his spot next to the major for this would have shown fear and submissive actions during a time of needed corporation. Francisco pulled the sedan back into the driveway and stopped just short of the main entrance to the main house. He exited the car and moved to the right of the car just in front of the spot where the major and Pietro were.

"Major, there hasn't been any seed dropped off this year and no mention of what crop we will be growing," remarked Pietro.

The major finished his wine and turned to Pietro. "Mr. Zucchet, there will not be any seed for your farm this year; you will grow the same crop you did last year and have the same quota. Will there be any problems?"

"There will be no problem with growing the same crop, Herr Major," answered Pietro, who was looking out into his fields and finishing his wine.

"Make sure you tell all the other farms that they will do the same," replied the major, who handed Pietro his empty wine glass. Pietro watched as they pulled out of the driveway and headed towards town.

* * *

As the day closed, Pietro was outside having his evening smoke and coffee when his son came around the corner looking better than the last time he saw him. He was walking better and without a limp.

"I noticed that you are not as hurt as the Germans thought you were, in fact, your limp is gone," said Pietro to his son, who had a smile on his face.

"Always let them think you are hurt more than you are or they will work you harder. I learned that working on the railroad," remarked Bruno as he started coughing into a handkerchief. Pietro noticed it had a bloodstain on it.

"How long have you been coughing up blood, son?" asked Pietro.

Bruno continued to cough and then looked up into the sky as planes moved across the sky.

"So, whose planes are over us?" asked Bruno.

"I really don't know, but what I do know is that they are going in the opposite direction, which means the Germans are going to get some visitors," answered Pietro with a smile on his face. He put his arm around his son. "It's good to have you home again," said Pietro with a tear in his eye.

Chapter 14

THE SIGNAL

IN THE SUMMER OF 1943, Italy was going through major changes throughout the country, which meant that their fortunes worsened. Benito Mussolini, who was arrested, and his Fascist government were put out of power by King Victor Emmanuel and replaced by Marshal Pietro Badoglio. The new government signed an armistice with the Allies, but there was still a very strong support for Mussolini, particular in northern Italy. The whole region was in turmoil, especially those parts that were run by the Fascists government. The Allied invasion of Sicily brought the war to the nation's very doorstep. The Italian home front was also in bad shape as the Allied bombings were taking their toll. Factories all over Italy were brought to a virtual standstill due to a lack of raw materials, as well as coal and oil. Additionally, there was a chronic shortage of food, and what food was available was being sold at nearly tripled prices.

***

Pietro and Bruno were again making more discoveries of raids on the farm's crops, including his extra land that previously was never discovered by the Germans. Pietro never could understand why someone would chop crops down that were not ready for consumption, but if you're desperate for food you'll do anything.

The farming area in this region was getting raided on a daily basis, and farmers were left to fend for themselves. Pietro decided that there needed to be more aggressive protection on the farmlands or they would be decimated before any of the crops could be harvested, not to mention their homes would be looted clean once the crops were gone. He knew that asking Francisco, who he had not seen since Mussolini was arrested, or the Germans was a waste of time. Bruno was sent out to the other farmers inviting them to a meeting at the auction house to discuss how to protect their lands from constant looting. Pietro had stopped having meetings at his barn for fear of being accused of being a rebel, plus the bombings were happening more frequently on meeting areas reported to the allies by local spies.

The auction house was sitting idle, which made it the perfect meeting area. Most farmers were told that this was their annual meeting to discuss next year's crop. On the day of the meeting, Pietro decided to ride his bike into town with Bruno staying behind to make sure the farm wasn't being looted while he was gone.

As he approached the outskirts of town he noticed a bright light in the distance. It was a signal being sent with a mirror reflecting the sun. Pietro stopped to take notice, then realized who was signaling him in the distance. He returned the signal with a mirror that he carried for such occasions. As he pulled up to the auction house, he could see that there were quite a few farmers outside waiting. Pietro knew just about all the farmers gathered.

"Good afternoon everyone, how are we all doing this great day? Have we heard our bombings for the day yet?" asked Pietro as he made his way past everyone and into the auction house. Inside, it was apparent there were different ideas about how to go about saving their lands from the ongoing looting. Before convening the meeting, Pietro scanned the room to make sure there wasn't a spy among them.

"Everyone knows why we are here today. Our country is being pulled into two different directions right now and you could be for one direction or the other direction. None of that matters because all of our lands are being looted. We need to come up with a plan for some type of security or we will have nothing left when this war is resolved. So, let's start out by listening to some of the ideas we have here."

There was a pause for about a minute and then someone stood to speak.

"We are feeding the Germans with most of our crops, so they should be the ones protecting our lands," remarked the farmer.

Another added, "We are also feeding the Fascists, so they should be protecting our lands and homes, too.

"We haven't seen either of them in quite some time," remarked another farmer.

"How long do you think it will be before the Allies start bombing our lands? They have already taken out most of the factories and even the silk factory in town," said another.

After more debate, a consensus formed. The farmers were on their own and needed to protect themselves, perhaps with some help from local police who could be trusted. As Pietro was leaving the auction house, his old friend Greg was waiting for him at the entrance smoking a cigarette. Pietro decided to stop and take some time to be with his friend and watch all the farmers leave the area. As the last ones left this very familiar area, Pietro looked at his friend and said, "He is here, and we need to go meet him when it gets dark."

Pietro, Greg, and the other farmers looked out of place in their farm clothes. Others milling around the streets, bars, and hat stores that were open were better dressed. Pietro didn't want to attract the attention of German and Italian soldiers in town.

"It's time for us to go and get this done. I want to get home sometime tonight," Pietro said. As Greg and Pietro got on their bikes a couple of Germans pointed in their direction and started heading towards them. Pietro noticed them and turned his bike in the opposite direction to avoid any problems. A German soldier rushed towards Greg and grabbed at the back of the bike, but Greg peddled hard and escaped. Pietro slowed down to allow his friend to catch up and to make sure he was all right.

"You okay?" asked Pietro.

"Yes, I am fine. Now let's get out of here before they catch us and take our bikes," replied Greg.

Pietro wanted to visit the apartment building where his mother had lived. He hadn't been there in quite some time and wanted to check his stash of food.

Pietro placed the key in the front door and could see movement inside the apartment. As he opened the door he saw a rather large man looking out the window. He then looked to his right and into the dining room and there was Gino.

"What took you so long?" Gino said with a broad smile. "This is Giacomo, he is going with me to Yugoslavia. We needed a place to hide, so we came here. I remembered that it was empty and thought it would be safe.

"So what is in Yugoslavia?" asked Pietro.

"There are a lot of soldiers heading to the north to regroup and start fighting the Germans. Besides there is work in Yugoslavia if the rebellion doesn't take hold and I need to go to work at the shipyards. We can hide out there and not be noticed with the other workers. How are Catherina and the girls doing?" asked Gino.

"They are doing great, and Catherina misses you very much," replied Pietro. Gino wanted to see his wife and daughters but knew it was too dangerous for them.

"The Allies have already landed down south and are making their way up North. There are rumors that Mussolini has been arrested and that the royal family has made an agreement with the Allies to end this war," Pietro said. "Is that true?"

"Yes, but the Germans are still a problem. They're arresting or killing defectors or anyone who is harboring them as well. That is why I won't come to the farm anymore and you cannot tell anybody you have seen me. I want this war over, Pietro. I want to be with my wife and children. I want us all to be free of this madness."

Chapter 15

TROOPS HARVEST CROPS

MUSSOLINI WAS PLACED BACK into power in Northern Italy after the Germans rescued him. He established his Fascist government again, which brought Francisco out of hiding and back into the farmers' lives. Things were different now and Francisco was more of a driver and interpreter who had no power. Most of his bodyguards were gone and so was his ambition to become royalty. He seemed to just want to survive the next day like everyone else.

The Germans didn't wait for Bruno to report for his usual railroad duties; they came early and got him this year. When Bruno asked about what timeframe he would be back one of the soldiers pointed a gun at him and told him to be quiet and get on the transport truck. Bruno's health hadn't improved. He was just as thin as he was when he came back to the farm in the spring. Pietro and Anna were devastated to see their son hauled away like a prisoner.

"Bruno is very sick and hasn't gained any weight this time," remarked Pietro.

"I know that and it scares me," Anna said.

"I don't think Bruno is going to last very long; that might be the last time we see our second son," Pietro said, holding back tears.

"I'm worried about Chester, too," she said. "We haven't seen or heard from him in over a year. The Germans are destroying this family!"

Pietro just stood and looked at his wife as she continued to finish the dishes and then turned around and walked out of her kitchen crying and visibly shaking.

**

Anna and Catherina helped out as much as they could, but the field work was very hard and with four small children running around it made matters more difficult. There wasn't any work available for Anna and Catherina since the silk and leather factories were bombed and destroyed by the Allies. The time on the farm seemed to slow down, with every day being harder than the next. Even the farm's hidden resources were dwindling with each passing day. The days of going to the markets in town were long gone and with the German and Italian soldiers raiding the farm on a regular basis meant that meals were reserved for the children. The weather was also getting ready to turn, which meant that the crops were getting ready to be harvested. Pietro had never harvested alone and decided to ask his longtime friend Greg for help. Greg was in the same situation because his sons were taken as well, so they both pooled their resources. Without their sons, it was two old men and a couple of worn-out horses.

As Pietro was getting the horse ready for the harvest time, he looked out into the distance and could see the familiar dust cloud coming his way. It was very early in the morning, and he was the only one up and decided not to wake the whole house. He went towards the main house, passing the new pens of geese, hogs, and turkeys that he started this summer. He took his position in front of the main door as he waited for the cars to pull into his driveway. Just as the first car rolled into the driveway, Pietro could already see it was Major Klein and Francisco followed by a troop transport and an empty truck. There were a couple of German soldiers but most of the other soldiers were Italian, but they weren't caring guns. In fact, they looked like they were more prisoners—not soldiers.

Catherina had heard the vehicles approach and quickly went to the kitchen to prepare the now customary snack for the

German officer. Just as the major was stepping out of his car, Pietro heard the familiar sound of his daughter coming out of the main house. She was ready with wine and hazelnuts. Pietro looked behind his daughter to see that all the children—they all looked they just got out of bed—were sitting on their assigned steps. He could hear Anna in the kitchen, which put a slight smile on his face as he returned his attention to their unscheduled guests. As Major Klein approached the main house, Pietro noticed that this wasn't the same man that he usually interacted with in the past. For the first time, Pietro noticed that he looked shaken, almost in fear.

"We are going to harvest your fields for you today and tomorrow, you will be expected to help. The food is needed very quickly in our mother land," the major said. Pietro didn't say a word and just nodded.

The major ordered the men to work. The German soldiers guarded the Italians, who were escaped soldiers and now German prisoners as Pietro had suspected. Pietro told Catherina to go back inside the house and lock all the doors. These soldiers looked like they haven't had a good meal in sometime, or a woman. Pietro wasn't taking any chances with his family. As they walked towards the barn, Pietro was wondering how they would be able to get all this work done in such a short time.

Major Klein drove off but left Francisco to ensure that the Italian soldiers performed their duties or be shot by the Germans guarding them. *Every one of the soldiers knows what they were doing*, thought Pietro. They grabbed the horse, cow, spade, and all the other equipment needed to start taking down the crops. Francisco walked over to Pietro and said, "They were all farmers at one time or another."

"Then why are they here and not fighting against the Allies?" asked Pietro.

"These soldiers have decided that they are on the wrong side and don't want to fight for the Axis Powers anymore, so instead of killing them we are using them to gather up the crops for you and the other farmers in this region. Why don't you go back to the house and spend some time with your family," replied Francisco. "We don't need you."

Pietro looked at Francisco angrily. *Adding insult to injury*, he thought. Getting into a confrontation with him probably wasn't going to be a good idea, so Pietro decided to walk to the main house to talk with his wife.

Anna had opened up the window in the kitchen and was listening to what was going on.

"So what are you going to do?" asked Anna. Pietro took the cup of coffee and sipped it.

"Well I am going to watch these fine young men work my fields and then we are going to feed them when they get done," answered Pietro.

"Pietro, we don't have the food to feed all of those boys, and they are not our responsibility," responded Anna.

"If my Italian son was working the fields somewhere and he looked like one of those boys we would want him to have a good meal. That is the least we can do for these Italian boys. The Germans will probably work them to death, so let's give them a decent meal on this farm," Pietro said.

Anna called Catherina from the other side of the house to help get the food ready so their guests would have a hot meal before they left that afternoon.

Pietro spent the day watching the soldiers harvesting his crops. He decided to see if they had any new technics for harvesting, but at the end of the day he saw nothing but a bunch of tired soldiers plowing his fields. It was getting dark when Francisco ordered the men to stop working. The two German soldiers walked over to the main road to look for the transport truck while Francisco stayed with the soldiers and Pietro. Much of the field was done but they would have to come back tomorrow and finish. Pietro usually took a week or more to finish harvesting the fields with Bruno, so watching these soldiers almost finish in a day was impressive. As the soldiers gathered around the barn to wait for their transport to arrive, Pietro made his way towards Francisco.

"Francisco, your prisoner soldiers almost finished in one day. I have never seen that happen."

"Well, we wanted to finish today but we will have to come back tomorrow," replied Francisco.

"Can I show you something over here in the fields which could help you the next time you come here, or if you do another field?" asked Pietro.

Anna was watching from the kitchen window and knew
what to do when she saw the two walk towards the fields, she
walked out of the side door with rations of polenta and sausage,
wrapped in a kitchen towel, to feed the Italian soldiers. The
soldiers saw Anna coming out the side of the main house but
made no attempt to go towards her for fear of being shot. As
Anna made her way towards the barn, Catherina walked out the
front of the house and started to sweep the front porch. As Anna
approached the barn, she looked behind her to ensure Catherina
was blocking the guard's view of the barn and soldiers. Anna
quickly distributed the food to the Italian soldiers so as not to
be noticed by the guards and Francisco. The soldiers took all the
food and quickly hid them within their ragged soldier's uniforms
and thanked Anna for her hospitality. She continued her travels
towards the other side of the barn to inspect the chicken, goose,
and duck coops to ensure none of their animals were missing.
Just as she was finishing she could see Pietro walking Francisco
back towards the barn area.

"So, like I was saying earlier, you need to plow in the
direction of how the crop was planted and not in the direction
you did today," Pietro told Francisco.

"Yes, I heard you for the third time, Mr. Zucchet. Is there
anything else you would like to advise me on before we get out
of here?" responded Francisco as he made a pointing gesture
towards his driveway.

"What time are you coming back tomorrow?" asked Pietro.

"Same time as this morning but we should be finished before
noon," replied Francisco.

***

The next morning they arrived at the same time as the
previous morning. But this morning, however, there was an
additional truck with the troop transport. Pietro figured that
they were going to load the entire harvested crop onto the other
truck and be done with his farm.

Pietro was already outside sitting in his normal spot having
his morning coffee. As the soldiers were being unloaded, each one
of them walked by Pietro and said, "Good morning, Mr. Zucchet,
and thank you for your hospitality." Francisco heard all of them

greet Pietro but couldn't figure out why they were so nice to him. Francisco dismissed the event and quickly put the soldiers back to work plowing the fields. This time the transport truck wasn't going anywhere and there was an additional German soldier watching. Pietro had already told Anna to have lunch ready for the soldiers, but now he was rethinking his generosity.

"Why do you have such a worried look on your face, Mr. Zucchet?" asked Francisco as he lit his cigarette.

"I just don't want my horse and cow to get over worked. This is a lot of work for them in a short period of time," answered Pietro. Just as he was finishing talking with Francisco, Pietro could hear the horse making noise from the barn. The soldiers were trying to get the horse to come out of the barn and he wasn't having anything to do with going out into the fields today. Pietro and Francisco walked over to the barn and sure enough the horse was kicking and pulling back on the reins. Pietro walked over to the soldiers.

"Please, give me the reins of my horse before he hurts you." Pietro grabbed the reins of the horse and proceeded to bring the horse out of the barn. "Francisco, I will have to help you today or the horse will not cooperate with the soldiers. He is not familiar with what is going on and will be very difficult all day." The soldiers turned their attention to the cow with no problem. Francisco had no choice but to do as Pietro requested; he had to get the crops into the truck today or face Major Klein.

Anna looked out the window and could see what was happening. She was smiling because she knew the horse wasn't going to be very cooperative today. Then her attention shifted on how she was going to feed all those boys today with all of the guards looking at what was going on in the farm today.

It was about eleven o'clock when Pietro and the soldiers finished up with the crops. Pietro completely forgot about the other area that needed to be harvested, and he wasn't sure if Francisco knew about that area or not, but he wasn't going to say anything. As Pietro made his way back to the barn where Francisco was standing, Anna came out to him with some water and something to eat.

"How are you doing?" asked Anna to her husband.

"I am fine, but the horse is done for the day," replied Pietro.

Anna was breaking up the food and giving it to her husband when Francisco moved towards the Italian soldiers sitting down taking a break by the front of the house. They were using the water pump to cool off and drink before heading back into the fields and load the crops up.

"Tell one of the Italian soldiers that there is a sack in the troop carrier with some polenta and sausage that has found its way under the back bench on the right-hand side," Anna said to her husband as she finished giving him the last of his lunch.

"You always find a way, my dear," remarked Pietro as he kissed his wife.

It was getting late in the evening when all of the crops were finally loaded on the truck. Pietro had given his wife's message to the oldest soldier he could find and the one he had spoken to the most. They were all stripped of their ranks so it was hard to see who was the leader of the Italian soldiers. As the soldiers were loaded on the truck, they all waved goodbye to the Zucchet family and Francisco took his usual place in the passenger seat.

"They are so worried about being punished and losing this war that they aren't paying attention," Pietro said of the Germans. "We will wait a couple of days for the animals to recover and then we will go harvest the other land and hide that crop for our own use."

Chapter 16

NAZIS TAKEOVER

IT WAS THE WINTER of 1944, and the Allies were trying to push their way through Italy. Northern Italy was still in control of Germany and Fascist supporters of Mussolini, who was put back into power by the Germans after he was arrested. The rest of Italy was now under control of the royal family and a new prime minister. The Axis Powers were slowly losing their control of Europe with every passing day. In addition, they were losing thousands of men to the new Italian freedom fighters out of Yugoslavia and the Alpine Mountain regions.

***

Catherina was outside playing with her two daughters to see if she could get them to expel some of their energy. Having two small children in an already small farmhouse was enough to make the most patient person lose their temper. There hadn't been a lot of activity on the farm since her father harvested the crop from their hidden area back in the fall timeframe. Catherina helped her father during that week, which wasn't all that bad. They did all the work at night so they were not discovered. They finished in four days and had enough to fill all of their pots with extra to sell in town.

As she played with Maria and Loretta, her thoughts drifted back and forth between her brothers and husband as she stared at the enormous Alpine Mountains in the background of the farm. She knew that Chester was in Germany somewhere being used as a force laborer since he had refused to fight for the Germans and Fascist puppets. Bruno was working for the Germans as a railroad laborer, but with the constant bombings from the Allies on their railroad system and him being constantly sick, she wondered if he would last until the summer. The reports on the conditions that they endured usually ended with them dying from sickness or being shot for not doing what they were told. But her greatest fear was for her husband, Gino. He had disappeared from Rome before the fighting between the Germans and Italians erupted after the armistice with the Allies was signed. The Germans had already come to the farm looking for him because he was suspected of other activities in Rome before he left. Her father had told her about seeing Gino in town, against Gino's advice, and his plans to escape to Yugoslavia. She hoped he made it and was safely milling among shipyard workers as planned.

She had visited Cimpello many times this winter looking for news about her husband and work. Each time she went to town she noticed that the conditions were getting worse, so work was impossible to find and there wasn't any news about her husband or any other deserter that she could find. The only news that was posted in the center of Cimpello was the same, which was that the Great Mussolini was back in power. The list of deserters that were captured and imprisoned was getting larger by each visit, but she did not see Gino's name.

As Catherina headed back to the main house from chasing her two daughters, she could see Pietro moving around in the barn. Anna was at the entrance of the house to greet her two granddaughters and warm them up with extra blankets.

"What is father doing?" asked Catherina to Anna.

"He needs some alone time and is going to town to read the latest news and see if there are any goods for sale," answered Anna. Before Anna could finish talking, Catherina was already heading towards the barn to talk with her father.

Pietro was getting his bike ready for the trip into town. He needed to get going before the weather and darkness got worse. Just as he stepped out of the barn, there was his oldest daughter staring at him.

"So what are you going to go do in town?" asked Catherina to her father.

"Well I am going to see if there are any supplies that we need and probably go to the café for a coffee or some wine," replied Pietro.

"What else are you going to do?" asked Catherina.

Pietro started to laugh and replied, "I am going to go around and ask to see if there is any news about Gino and the freedom fighters from up north. If I get any information I will be sure to come share it with you, my dear," replied Pietro to his daughter as he kissed her goodbye.

Pietro was just about to be in town when he noticed German cars and trucks. They were everywhere and it seemed that they were looking for someone or something. He thought that he should turn around and go back home, but the Germans already saw him. If he had turned around then they would have suspected him of being guilty of something, so he decided to continue his trip into the middle of town for the latest news. He could see the German soldiers yelling at people in stores, on the street, and in their homes while they held some type of lists in their hands. It was very chaotic and dangerous, so he made his way as quickly as possible. After Pietro dropped his bike in front of the steps that he had climbed countless times in the past, he could already tell that there wasn't any new news posted at the top. He almost turned around and got on his bike but he decided to make the long hike up the stairs to read the latest old news. Just as he got closer, there was something new posted on the board which caught his eye. Pietro got to the top of the stairs so he could view the notice which read: *Any person or family knowingly hiding or not telling authorities the whereabouts of known deserters will be subject to harsh punishments which includes imprisonment, loss of property, or even death.*

Pietro got on his bike and decided that today wasn't a good day to be in town. As he made his way through town, he could still see that the soldiers were still harassing everyone. Pietro wanted to check on his apartment, go to the market, and maybe go see about a coffee but none of that was going to happen. Just as Pietro was about to make his last turn out of town, he could see a checkpoint that had been set up since he entered the town. The soldiers asked the couple in front of him what their names were and if they knew of any deserters in the area. They were checking the couple's names from a list. After a short period the couple was granted permission to continue their travels. It was Pietro's turn so he approached the soldiers.

"What is your name, and where do you live?" asked the soldier who didn't want to be there but spoke perfect Italian.

"My name is Pietro Zucchet, and I live on my farm just outside the town."

The soldier who didn't even look in Pietro's direction went immediately to his list to see if he could find Pietro's name. After a short time, the soldier ordered, "Stay here, and I will be right back." The soldier walked towards the same Gestapo Captain who came to his house with Bruno not too long ago. After a brief conversation, the soldier returned to Pietro.

"Where are your son's Bruno and Chester, and have you seen them?"

Pietro was wondering why they didn't ask about Gino.

"Both of my sons are working for Germany right now. Do you have any information about their whereabouts?" asked Pietro.

"What do they do for Germany?" asked the soldier who ignored Pietro's request.

"My son Bruno is working on rebuilding the railroads, and Chester is in Germany working for your government, but I'm not too sure what he is doing exactly," replied Pietro.

"Are these people still living on the farm?" asked the soldier as he handed Pietro the list. Pietro looked at the list and everyone on the farm was listed with the exception of Bruno.

"Everyone is still on the farm and Bruno lives there as well when he comes back in the spring to help me with the crops." The soldier made a notation on the paper and then looked at his superior who waved in their direction.

"You can go, Mr. Zucchet."

Pietro didn't even hesitate and started to pedal his bike as quickly as his tired old legs would allow him before they decided to ask questions about Gino. Pietro was about to reach his final destination of the day and could see the farm ahead of him. He finally slowed his pedaling down after pushing his bike down the dirt road as quickly as he could move it when he heard some commotion from where the checkpoint was set up. He stopped pedaling and looked behind him to just hear a woman screaming, and then he heard a gun fire. Then there was silence where screaming was heard just a second earlier. Pietro lowered his head to pray for the unfortunate ones that just lost their lives.

Just as he got off his bike and started to walk his bike through the stone driveway, Anna came out.

"Did you hear gunfire?"

Pietro nodded. "It is not safe to go back into town anytime soon."

Chapter 17

HORSE AND CARTS

THE WAR WAS A lost cause for the Germans, but they still believed that there was hope through intimidation and fear. Even the children were not allowed to go to school anymore or be away from an adult if they were outside or visiting other families. Pietro would make his rounds to the other farmers to see what news he could get from them, but they too were not venturing into the towns anymore. The bombings were getting louder and more frequent as the months passed with heavy smoke being trapped in the valley for days. The Ally bombings concentrated on industrial areas and the railroads but left most of the planting fields alone, which helped most of the farmers survive. The ground war had not made it to this area, but it was only a matter of time due to limited amounts of roads available for this area. What worried Pietro the most was if the Allies wanted the Venice area they would have to travel through his region to get there, which meant destruction. The other possible invasion area could come through Yugoslavia, but that would mean the Russians would come and Pietro feared them the most. They hated Italy ever since the Russian Invasion.

It was getting warmer and the planting season was just around the corner. Pietro was up early as usual with many chores ahead of him. The smartest thing they did was getting the coops ready for the different birds and rotating them from the barn so they would always have a few in a safe place. Luckily, they had enough food to survive the winter and well past the spring. But money was running out. As Pietro worked his chores, he heard strange noises coming from the valley that sounded as though there were animals being tortured. Pietro looked in the barn and could see that the animals were very unsettled and nervous.

As he glanced over at the main house, he could see Anna with her head out the window looking in the direction of the sounds that he heard earlier. Pietro turned around and got his bike before he shut the doors to the barn. He headed back to the main house with his bike in tow.

"Where are all those noises coming from, Pietro?" asked Anna with Catherina standing next to her helping with the morning dishes.

"It sounds as though someone is forcing the animals to do something they don't want to and some yelling from people," answered Pietro.

"I have never heard anything like that before except at the auction house or the butler shop."

"I am going to go see what is going on, and I want you all to make sure you are ready for any visitors while I am gone," replied Pietro.

"They are coming here."

Pietro looked outside and could see the cloud of smoke. The women knew what was expected and started to get the children in place and get the necessary refreshments ready for their visitors. Pietro made his way to the front of the house, but not before he moved his bike out of sight so nobody knew that he was getting ready to go for a ride. As Pietro sat down on the bench to wait for his visitors, he could already tell that this was going to be a very large convoy. The noises he was hearing earlier were starting to get louder as the vehicles got closer. For the first time, he was unsure of what to expect.

Francisco went just past the turn into the Zucchet farm before he stopped to let his passenger out of the vehicle. It was this time of the year that Major Klein made his rounds to check on the farming situation in this region; however, he wasn't the passenger in Francisco's vehicle. Francisco opened the door

of the vehicle to let out the Gestapo captain who had replaced
Major Klein. Francisco looked down the rocky driveway to see
Pietro staring in his direction, and at the same time he watched
the animal transporter turn into the driveway.

Pietro could see the very large truck full of animals back
into his driveway and knew what was about to happen. There
was also a bus that stopped just short of the driveway full of
people, mostly young Italians, who Pietro feared were going to
be used as laborers, or worse, be sent to concentration camps.
The noises that Pietro and Anna had heard earlier were the ones
coming from the bus and transport.

"Anna, stay in the house with Catherina and the children.
Lock the doors and don't let anybody in the house until I say
so or they break the doors down," ordered Pietro. Anna quickly
turned around and did what she was commanded. She looked
towards the steps and to her amazement Catherina had already
set the children down on their assigned steps. Anna quickly sat
down next to the first step and her youngest son, he was the last
of her sons and she was going to protect him even if it meant
her life. Catherina quickly walked into the kitchen to make sure
all the doors were locked. After she made sure everything was
locked, she couldn't help but look out the kitchen window to
see the bus full of people. She stopped to look and see who was
on the bus and in the back looking out towards her was one of
her best friends, Maria, who was yelling for her to come out and
speak to her.

***

German soldiers exited the truck with their rifles by their
sides.

"Good morning, Herr Captain, what can I do for you, and
will Major Klein be joining us today?" asked Pietro.

"Mr. Zucchet, our records show that you have some animals
and equipment that your country will need for the time being,
with the promise that you will get them back or will be reimbursed
with monetary funds at a later date."

As the captain was talking, Francisco was filling out some
paperwork for Pietro as soldiers headed towards his barn. Pietro
started to walk in the direction of the barn.

"What are you taking from me? I have to plant my fields and how can I plant if you take all of my equipment?" asked Pietro, looking at the captain who was walking with him towards the barn. "Does Major Klein know that this is going on?"

"Major Klein is no longer attached to this region, you will be answering to me," replied the captain. Pietro took a couple more steps and knew that he had better stop walking or he might not live the rest of the day. The captain upholstered his Lugar.

Catherina was watching through the kitchen window when her mother decided to join her.

"What is going on?" asked Anna.

"It looks like they are going to take the horse and cow from us," answered Catherina.

Pietro was watching the soldiers go into the barn and the first thing they took out was his beloved cart.

"How am I going to transport my crops to the auction house if you take my cart?" asked Pietro.

"Mr. Zucchet, according to my records we have harvested your crops for the last two years, so there is no need for you to have this cart," replied the captain. The soldiers moved the cart to the side of the barn and then emerged with the horse. After about a minute, the horse was loaded onto the truck without too much resistance.

Anna looked at her eldest daughter.

"Grab all of the children and come out to the barn right now!" Catherina only saw her mother excited a few times and this was one of them and she did as she was told. Anna made her way out of the kitchen through the side door towards the barn. Catherina went to the steps and picked up her youngest daughter, grabbed her oldest daughter by her hand, and then told her two siblings to follow her out the kitchen door towards an uncertain situation.

The captain heard the door open and turned to see Anna coming in his direction. Pietro turned at the same time to see her heading in his direction. The captain waved at one of the soldiers standing next to the truck. The soldier moved to block Anna from coming any closer to the barn.

"Anna, go back into the house!" yelled Pietro. Just as Pietro was yelling at his wife, Catherina emerged with all the children in tow and headed in the same direction as Anna. Anna stopped just before the soldier so as not to make matters worse. Pietro was just about to make his way towards his wife when he heard some more movement from the barn. The soldiers were coming out of the barn with their only cow. Pietro froze in his steps not knowing which direction to move.

"Herr Captain, please don't take the cow. It is our only source of milk for this whole family," responded Anna. The captain looked at Anna just as Catherina and all of the children reached her side. Anna reached for Maria, picking her up and then turning so the captain could see all of the children.

"Mr. Zucchet, can you use the cow to plow your fields?" asked the captain.

"Yes, I can use the cow to plow my fields," responded Pietro. The captain turned around and motioned the soldiers to stop loading the cow. The soldiers stopped moving the cow onto the truck and handed the rope around the cow's neck to Pietro.

"Thank you, Captain," responded Anna.

"I am not giving you the cow for the milk but to make sure the fields get plowed to harvest this year's crop," replied the captain. He entered his car and the convoy hustled away down the gravel road, undoubtedly heading to another farm.

***

"Why are you smiling, Dad? They just took your horse and cart," asked Catherina.

"My dear, I am very sad they took the horse and cart but very happy that they took them because this isn't the first time I have seen the Germans take animals and carts," answered Pietro.

"What do you mean?" asked Catherina.

"During my war, when the Germans started to take animals and carts, they were about to lose the war. It is a desperate attempt to replenish their existing supplies and the last-ditch effort before defeat. Now I have to go hug your mother because if she had not come out with the children, I probably would have had to but the plow blade on my back to get the fields done," answered Pietro. Catherina watched her father walk back to the main house with an extra skip in his step.

Chapter 18

PARATROOPERS

IN THE SUMMER OF 1944, with the Allied forces nearby, the partisan resistance (Italian Resistance against the Germans and Pro-Fascist Mussolini's) in Italy staged an uprising against the Germans and Pro-Fascist supporters. German casualties from the Italian partisans in the mountain regions surrounding the Zucchet farm were in the thousands. The Italian Resistance unfortunately suffered casualties far exceeding the Germans and Pro-Fascist supporters due to their lack of war-fighting capabilities and lack of guns and ammunition.

***

Pietro was coming back from his daily trip of checking on the crops, visiting other farmers, and a quick tour of the town to see if there was any new information on what was going in the region and the war. As he approached the gravel driveway, he dismounted from the bike to walk the rest of the way. He noticed that Catherina was outside playing with her daughters.

"So, how was your bike ride today?" asked Catherina as her father bent down to hug both of his granddaughters.

"It was fine, nothing has changed since yesterday, and hopefully everyone is busy trying to kill each other so they will let our crops alone," replied Pietro.

"Maria, go take Loretta back inside the house and see if Nona will give you something to eat," ordered Catherina to her oldest daughter. Maria grabbed Loretta by the hand and guided her young sister back into the house. After Catherina made sure the girls went into the house, she followed her father to the barn to see what he really found out during his bike ride. They were very careful not to share too much information in front of the young children for fear of them telling the Germans during their visits. The Germans were very good at getting information from any source, including the use of young children who were taught to tell the truth when asked by an adult.

"Dad, what else did you find out during your ride?" asked Catherina as she entered the barn. Pietro turned around to see that his daughter was alone.

"Shut the door just in case the girls come running back or your brother or sister come running in here and we don't see them," replied Pietro. Catherina did as her father told her.

"So what did you find out about Gino, Chester, and Bruno?" asked Catherina.

"This is what I can tell you. Gino is probably in Yugoslavia either fighting against the Germans or working at the shipyards, but he is not coming home until the war is over. That is all I could find out. There is no word about Bruno except that he is still working the railroad detail and Chester is still in Germany working," replied Pietro. "All the people that the Germans rounded up and imprisoned in the auction house have been sent away to concentration camps in Germany," remarked Pietro as he watched his daughter's expression turn to horror. She knew that all of her friends and people she had grown up with that were at the auction house were never going to come back.

"You mean everyone is gone from the auction house? They are all gone?" asked Catherina.

"Yes, my dear, everyone is gone from the auction house. There are more Germans in town than I have ever seen so we need to stay away as much as possible," answered Pietro.

Catherina looked at her father and asked, "Why are there so many Germans in town? We have nothing here of importance, we are just a farming region."

"My dear, the partisan resistance has been killing a lot of

Germans as of late, and with the Allies coming up the coast the Germans are desperately trying to stop their advancement and beat back the partisans. We need to stay out of everyone's way or this farm and this family will exist no more. Now let's go inside the house and have some dinner."

***

As the evening wore on and dinner was finished, Pietro made his way out to his familiar seat out in the front for his evening smoke and coffee. Anna and Catherina were in the kitchen cleaning up the dinner mess and then they would get the children and grandmother ready for bed. As the sun was working its way down, Pietro was looking out in his fields and watching this year's crop moving with every gust of wind coming from Mother Nature. Then from the distance he could hear planes coming from the south. This wasn't normal so he moved from his seat to go see what types of planes were coming in the direction of his farm. Just as he was moving towards the barn, Anna was looking out of the kitchen window to see what the planes were doing.

"Lock up the house and get the kids ready to sit on the steps, this doesn't sound like normal fighter planes," ordered Pietro to his wife. Anna didn't even answer her husband; she just closed the shudders of the kitchen windows and proceeded to get the children ready for some visitors.

Pietro looked up into the sky as he cleared the main house. The planes were dropping paratroopers, and they were German. They were falling all over the area surrounding the farm. Pietro counted five planes dropping hundreds of paratroopers and they were fully armed. He checked the barn to make sure it was all closed off and then headed back to the main house. As he entered the house he could hear the paratroopers landing in the fields. Pietro looked inside the house quickly.

"We are ready," yelled Anna at her husband. Pietro looked at her and could see that she was frightened and so were the children.

"Everything will be fine. I am going outside to greet our visitors. Don't move until you hear from me," replied Pietro. Pietro shut the door to the house and made his way to his chair.

He could see hundreds of Germans running towards the town and the woods; he knew that it would only be a matter of time before he had visitors.

Pietro heard the noise of the rocks from underneath the German soldier's boots as they made their way up his driveway. Pietro could see there were four soldiers coming his way, with a sergeant in front.

"How many people are in the house," yelled the sergeant.

Pietro yelled back, "There are three ladies and four children in the house."

The sergeant stopped in front of Pietro and ordered him to open the door so they could inspect the house and have everyone get out.

"Herr Sergeant, my mother has polio and is unable to get out of the bed on the second floor," answered Pietro as he opened the door and waved for everyone to come out of the house. Anna and the children came out, but Catherina refused to leave her grandmother alone so she went upstairs with the soldiers as they inspected the house.

"What are you looking for, Herr Sergeant?" asked Pietro.

"We are looking for partisans and any supporters. Are there any here?" asked the sergeant as he held his machine gun towards Pietro.

"We are only farmers, Herr Sergeant. I am too old for war and both my sons are already working for Germany," answered Pietro.

Catherina was upstairs sitting next to her grandmother, who was shaking from fear as the soldiers looked around the room for anything.

"Move the woman so we can inspect underneath the bed," ordered one of the soldiers as he pointed his gun towards Catherina.

"She is in a lot of pain every time she is moved and she is blind, there is nothing underneath the bed," responded Catherina. The soldier raised his weapon in a threatening manner, which made Catherina move very quickly to pick her grandmother up before the soldier decided to end both of their lives. The soldiers flipped the bed over to reveal nothing but a couple of children's wooden toys that Pietro had made for his grandchildren that went missing months ago. The soldiers left the upstairs room and went back outside.

Pietro was standing by Anna and the children when the soldiers came out of the house. "There is nobody in the house except one old woman and a young one," replied one of the soldiers to the sergeant.

"Go check the barn and the rest of the farm," ordered the sergeant to the soldiers that just came out of the house. Pietro noticed that the sergeant was getting very tired of not finding anything and upset that he wasn't running towards the town like the other paratroopers. The soldiers returned after about five minutes of searching the barn and the rest of the farm without finding anything suspicious. As the soldiers departed the farm, a German officer stood in the road waiting for the soldiers to come from the farm. The sergeant reported his findings to him as they headed towards town.

"What is going on?" asked Catherina.

"They are here to fight the Allies and put down the partisans resistance. I want everyone to stay here in case we have any more visitors. Do not leave the driveway."

Pietro walked towards the barn so he could get on the roof to see if there was a better view of what was happening. As he emerged on top of the barn, he could tell that half of the paratroopers were headed towards town and the other half were headed towards the wooded area at the base of the mountain range. He looked south to make sure there were no more paratroopers headed in their direction and noticed something odd about one of his corn stacks about a hundred feet from the house. There was a German paratrooper hiding behind one of them so as not to be noticed. Then Pietro could hear the planes coming again from the south, but these were not the paratrooper planes. He looked over the horizon to see that the sky was full of fighters and bombers headed towards the mountain range. As the planes flew over the farm, Pietro yelled back to everyone to get back into the main house. Then the bombing started at the base of the closest mountain range, which lit up the sky like a morning sunrise. Mortar shells, machine gun fires, and more bombings followed this. It lasted no more than thirty minutes, but Pietro could tell that the Germans knew exactly where the partisans were located. There was some isolated small arms fire but as the sun finished its decent, he could see most of the paratroopers headed back towards town from the mountain range. Pietro moved from the rooftop and headed towards the paratrooper with a pitch fork at the ready.

Pietro walked very slowly towards the soldier so as not to make matters any worse. He could hear something as he got closer but couldn't make it out, and then he realized the soldier was sobbing like a child. Pietro moved in front of the soldier who was holding his head with both of his hands over his ears. His rifle was on the ground next to him with a bayonet attached to one end of it. Pietro reached for the rifle just as the soldier raised his head to look at the farmer. The soldier did not try to stop Pietro from taking his rifle, but instead curled up in the fetal position and continued to cry. Pietro noticed that the soldier could not be older than fourteen years old.

"Wait here until I get back," replied Pietro in his best German.

Everyone was in the kitchen when Pietro walked in the side door towards the barn carrying the rifle.

"Make me a plate of dinner and some water," ordered Pietro. Everyone looked in horror as they noticed what he was carrying.

"What do you need with a plate of food?" asked Anna. Pietro was working the bayonet off the tip of the rifle when he answered his wife.

"There is a boy on our farm who is scared as hell and needs something to eat." Anna was defiant and refused to get up and get a plate of food ready.

"He is the enemy and I am not going to feed him!" she barked back. She just sat there looking at her grandchildren and children who were sitting and holding each other.

"If this was one of your sons, wouldn't you want him to be fed?" asked Pietro. Anna looked at her husband and got up to get the plate of food ready for their enemy visitor.

Pietro walked out to the soldier with the plate of food in one hand and the water in the other. The bayonet was at the ready in his front belt just in case, but he left the rifle back at the house.

When he approached the boy, he was still sobbing like a child that lost his mother. Pietro put the food and water down in front of him and left without saying anything. Pietro grabbed the rifle that was leaning against the house and proceeded towards the barn. He went inside the barn with the rifle and grabbed the tree axe. He leaned the rifle against the main post of the barn and then raised the axe to break the rifle into two pieces. Pietro emerged from the barn with both pieces of the rifle. He walked towards the fields and threw both pieces in different directions before he headed back to the main house.

Throughout the evening Pietro could hear gunfire coming from the distance. There were no more bombings from planes or mortar shells, which meant the Germans were finishing up what they started earlier in the evening. Pietro hoped that Gino wasn't anywhere close when they started to bomb, but only time would tell if he made it out. He was up all night sitting in the kitchen with the bayonet beside him just in case they had any visitors, but none came. The morning sun rose like it had every morning of Pietro's life, but this morning he was exhausted from the previous day's events. He made himself some coffee before anybody came to the kitchen. With his coffee in his hand he walked out of the house, into the morning dew and the smell of burning woods and war. The smell of war was one he had hoped he wouldn't have to experience again, but here it was at his doorstep. He headed towards their visitor to check on his status. Pietro walked very slowly so as not to disturb him but just as he was getting closer he could see that the plate was empty and so was the cup of water. Their visitor had departed, but Pietro could see that he headed in the opposite direction of the Germans from the look of the bent crops. He bent down to get the plate and cup before heading back to the house. Catherina was outside with a cup of coffee looking in the direction of the bombing. She shifted her attention towards her father as he approached her.

"So I guess he was hungry?" asked Catherina.

"Yes, it looks like he was. He also left in the opposite direction of his fellow soldiers, so be careful for the next couple of days just in case he comes back for another meal," responded Pietro as both of them started to laugh. It had been a long time since they enjoyed a laugh, just the two of them. Pietro grabbed his daughter and gave her a hug as best he could with the dishes and his coffee in his hand.

"Let's go inside and tell your mother that our visitor has

departed and get something to eat," replied Pietro as they both
started to walk towards the house, and Catherina grabbed the
dishes from her father. Catherina stopped just short of the house
and turned to her father to ask him a question.

"Do you think Gino was anywhere near that bombing area
yesterday?"

Pietro looked deep into his daughter's eyes. "No, dear, he is
in Yugoslavia. Now let's go inside." Pietro held the door open
for his daughter as he scanned the mountain and forest for any
signs. Just as he was turning towards the door he could see the
familiar flashing mirror just west of the area that was bombed.
He smiled as he turned his attention towards breakfast and the
possibility of some sleep.

Chapter 19

Nervous

AS THE MORNING sun began to rise, Betty was starting her day like so many others. She would ensure that Francisco's uniform was in perfect condition and that all of his seams were ironed straight. The evening coals from the fireplace were used in the iron for heat. She always refreshed and buffed the polish on his tall, black leather boots so another person could see their reflection. His leather belt and holster for his Beretta pistol also glimmered. The feather's in his hat were bright red and black and needed the occasional fluffing. She would lay out his uniform every morning to ensure he was the best dressed Fascist supporter of Mussolini.

Her dream of becoming a member of the royal family was a lost cause. But Betty stayed with Francisco for love and survival, for she knew that her life was in jeopardy if she left him. With no other family members that would help her, she worried what might happen if Francisco was killed or taken prisoner. Every time she brought up the possibility of Mussolini losing the war, he assured her that there was no way that was going to happen as long as the Germans were their allies.

Francisco was in the kitchen having his morning coffee and reading the latest propaganda newspaper about how the Axis Powers were holding off the Allies invasion of northern Italy when Betty entered.

"Would you like some breakfast this morning?" she asked as she looked around the kitchen to see what she could make him. There was only some old bread, honey, and a couple of cookies given to her by one of her friends. Francisco nodded that he wasn't hungry and that he needed to get going because today there was a rally that his uncle would be at in the city. This rally was going to lay out the plans for the Axis Powers next move towards fighting the Allies. Francisco went into the bedroom to finish dressing, distracted by his worries. Francisco didn't know who to trust, and for the first time since he joined the Fascist movement, he was scared that he may be killed by the Allies, or worse, by one of his own countrymen fighting for the Allies. He finished dressing and left the apartment without even saying goodbye to Betty.

She watched him leave the apartment while drying her hands with the kitchen towel, noticing that he had lost a lot of weight lately as he opened the door of his sedan. She looked down the road where he was headed and saw Germans standing at the roadblock. They had been there for about six months and were at least some protection from the people who wanted to end Francisco's reign over them. She watched Francisco take off in his sedan before she closed the window and went about her day as Francisco's live-in girlfriend.

As he drove past the roadblock and headed towards the Pordenone for the rally, Francisco noticed that the Germans were starting to load their trucks with their personal gear. *They must be ready to start their drive towards the south and defeat the Allies*, thought Francisco.

As Francisco drove into the town, he could see that there were a lot people from all over the region gathered. He smiled knowing that this was the start of turning the Allies back south and eliminating these pesky Alpine fighters from this area. He parked his car away from the crowds and started looking for his uncle. Francisco worked his way towards the podium like he had done dozens of times. The crowd didn't move away from him to allow access towards the front, instead there was a different element to the crowd one that caused him to be more cautious about his surroundings for the first time since joining the Fascist movement.

"So what is going on with all the other people here?" asked Francisco to the other Fascists in uniforms. They both looked at him and then themselves with a look of disbelief.

"You're kidding right?" answered one of the supporters who looked like he had not slept in a week. "Most of the Germans are leaving and going back to Germany because the Allies are getting ready to invade. We will be left here to defend ourselves against the Allies and any other anti-Axis Powers supporters," replied the supporter.

Francisco looked at him in disbelief and then started to look around to see the faces of the crowd. What he noticed made his neck hair's stand up; the fear in the eyes of the people was gone. Francisco started to look for his uncle more intensely, but he was nowhere to be seen. Just as he was getting ready to start his movement towards the front again, one of the supporters whispered, "Your uncle was taken prisoner by the Allies on his way here."

A German major walked up to the podium to start talking to the crowd. "We are here to celebrate our latest victory over the rebels to the north and the Allies to the south, both of which are on the run." The crowd started to celebrate and cheer for the Axis Powers but it wasn't as loud as previous rallies. The major waited for the crowd to settle down before he continued his speech. "I need all the Il Duce leadership members to come to the stage so we can all see the future of this great country of Italy," the major continued. Francisco and the other members wearing their uniforms worked their way up to the podium. As the members finished mustering in order behind the major, he started to shake each member's hand until he was in front of Francisco. He took Francisco's hand and leaned into him to whisper. "Stay on stage after I have all the other's leave so we can talk afterwards; we have a special assignment for you." The major finished shaking everyone's hand and went back to the podium.

"Ladies and Gentlemen, these are your leaders and will need your support in the near future to continue the hard work of the Axis Powers and complete the victory for Il Duce's Northern alliance with Germany. The Fuhrer has granted all the German soldiers in this region an extended stay back to the homeland to spend the upcoming winter months with our families. These great men behind me will be leading the small contingent force we will leave behind and, of course, follow the orders of ll Duce's higher command and control his forces in this region."

As he stood there listening to the major's propaganda, Francisco looked straight into the crowd. Instead of seeing rows of supporters, he saw crowds of confused masses who were doing more whispering than listening. The major finished his speech with the traditional salute in celebration to the Fuhrer, which was greeted with mixed audience participation. All of the II Duce leaders had left the stage. The major was talking with a mix of German and Italian soldiers, when he waved for Francisco to join them.

"Gentlemen, this is our new regional commander who will ensure that the local families and farmers are in compliance with our directives and supporting our industry as best as possible," said the major as he introduced Francisco to the military leaders, some of which he had already known from previous encounters. "Make sure you support him in his endeavors, especially with military personnel if he needs your assistance. Right now he will be escorted to his posted duties with my personnel. Thank you for coming out to the rally, and we will be in touch real soon about your uncle and further directions."

As Francisco pulled up to the auction house he could see that most, if not all, the Germans were gone. He stopped his sedan just short of the main office and could see that there were people inside and they looked like German soldiers. As he opened the door, he was startled by what he saw in the office. All the paperwork and books were missing from the shelves and every draw was opened and emptied. There were four soldiers sitting in the office. Three were privates and one a sergeant.

"Are you the new commander of this region?" asked the sergeant.

"Yes, I am. I was just told by the major that I would have some personnel available to help me," replied Francisco.

"Where do you live?' asked the sergeant.

"Just down the road, why?" asked Francisco.

"Take two of these privates and show them where you live and then come back tomorrow in the morning like you normally would and we will go from there," answered the sergeant.

The two privates looked like they couldn't be older than sixteen. "Okay, see you in the morning, Herr Sergeant," replied Francisco as he headed out the door with the two young German soldiers. Francisco got into his sedan and headed towards his apartment with the two soldiers following him in their military sedan. As he pulled up next to the entrance of his apartment complex, the soldiers pulled up behind him, exited their vehicle, and approached Francisco.

The eldest looking of the two asked him, "Where do you live?" Francisco pointed at the window on the second floor. "Is there another entrance into this building other than that one?" asked the soldier as he pointed at the main entrance.

"Nope, that is the only way into and out of this building," replied Francisco knowing there was another entrance but wanted to keep his options open just in case he needed to make a quick escape.

"We will set up our post here, and if you need anything just let us know ahead of time." Francisco smiled and headed into the building not sure if they were bodyguards, supporters, or if he was their prisoner. As Francisco walked the flight of stairs to his apartment, he concluded that it was time to have an exit strategy, which included Betty.

Chapter 20

VISITORS

THE SUMMER HAD PASSED and fall was around the corner. There had been little activity on the farm since the paratroopers raided it earlier in the summer. The days would begin with bombings and shootings from all sides of the farm. The fighting also spilled over into most nights. Pietro wouldn't allow any lights or fires at night for fear that the house or barn would be a target of an air bombing. No one was allowed to leave the farm, with the exception of Pietro who wouldn't even go to the town or city anymore for fear of being taken prisoner and sent to one of the slave or concentration camps. He was the only male on the farm and if he was taken the farm was sure to fall into the wrong hands. The Germans were getting desperate and started to take the elderly and the very young to be used as slave labor.

Pietro was looking at what few crops he had and knew it was time to start harvesting them. This would be a difficult period without any help from his sons. The Germans or Fascists hadn't even come out to check on the crops like they had in the past. Anna approached her husband as he looked into the crops from the front porch of the main house.

"What is on your mind?" asked Anna.

"Even when I get the fields harvested how am I going to get

the crops to the auction house?" asked Pietro. "The cart is gone and so is the horse."

"How about we get the crops harvested first and then figure out a way to get them to town," answered Anna.

"You're right, the crops need to be harvested first, and then we will work on getting them to town. I will check with the other farmers to see what they are going to do about getting their crops to town. We probably will need to pool our resources together or pray for some type of help," Pietro said as he started to walk towards the barn to get his gear ready for the cow.

That evening Anna was serving dinner with most of the family in the kitchen. Catherina was upstairs feeding her grandmother and getter her ready for bed. She also had Maria with her to help her out if she needed some assistance. As Anna served Pietro he remarked, "I have some farmers coming over this evening to discuss what we are going to do with our crops. It won't take long and everyone should stay in the house."

"Which farmers are coming over so I can get some food ready for them?" asked Anna.

Catherina was entering the kitchen and heard her mother's last request. "Who is coming over tonight?" asked Catherina. Pietro looked at his wife with stern eyes as if saying that he was upset that his eldest daughter heard him.

"There is no need to prepare food; this won't be a social engagement, just some wine and cheese will do fine. They will be here in about an hour and make sure that all the lights are out when it gets dark. Have Catherina bring the wine and cheese out to me," ordered Pietro as he finished his dinner.

Everyone had finished their dinner and was helping clear the table as Anna was getting the wine and cheese ready for the evening's guest. Maria was so much help now that she would follow her mother around all day long so she could have something to do and be her constant assistant. Anna was about ready to start the journey towards the barn when she remembered that Pietro wanted Catherina to bring the food and wine, she had an instinct as to why but kept to herself.

"Catherina, would you please take the food and wine to your father?" asked Anna.

"Maria and I will take all the wine and food to the barn."

Anna looked down at her oldest granddaughter and smiled at her as she gave her the tray of food. Catherina grabbed the basket of wine while guiding her oldest daughter towards the back door. They both walked very slowly towards the barn because it was getting dark and very hard to see. As they got closer to the barn, Catherina could hear voices coming from the barn, but as soon as they got closer the barn was quiet again. Pietro met them at the door and grabbed the food from Maria who was very excited about leaving the house. She started to pull on her grandfather so he would pick her up, which he did as he turned to put the food down on the table.

"Who were you talking with?" asked Catherina as she made her way into the dark barn.

"No one. I was talking to the cow, telling her that she has a lot of walking to do the next three to four days." Pietro smiled.

Catherina put the basket of wine down next to the food and started to look around the barn, but the only thing she could see were the cow and some chickens running around looking for food before it got too dark to eat.

"Why don't you go back into the house and let Maria stay here with me, I will bring her in when she settles down," ordered Pietro who always had a soft heart for his granddaughters. Catherina did as her father requested, but not before she gave her eldest a kiss good night. As Catherina was walking back to the house she heard something from behind her and she looked around to see that Mr. Martin was going into the barn.

Pietro was holding Maria and pouring himself some wine when Greg walked into the barn. Pietro turned to see his longtime friend and noticed that he was wearing a small jacket as it was starting to get cold at night.

"You want some wine?" asked Pietro. Greg smiled as if Pietro really had to ask him that question. As Pietro poured wine, he could hear the other farmers arriving at the barn for their meeting to figure out what to do with this year's crop.

Pietro decided that it was best to have at least one lantern on so they could see each other talk and find the wine and food. Everyone knew that if they heard an airplane the lantern would be turned out for fear of being bombed. Pietro put Maria down and walked to the middle of the barn to start the meeting.

Everyone stopped talking and shifted their attention to Pietro.

"Does anyone have a way of transporting our crops to town?" asked Pietro to the other farmers. There was silence in the room for about a minute before Pietro spoke again. "Has anyone been visited by the Germans or Fascists in the last three months about your crops?" Again nobody spoke. After a minute Greg grabbed the lantern and turned it down so it was out. The barn was pitch dark as the planes flew from east to west. Pietro could hear the familiar movement of feet from the back of barn near the cow coming towards the direction of the farmers. After the planes flew long enough that their engines were not in hearing distance of the barn, Greg lit the lantern and revealed two more bodies in the barn.

"We will help you with your crops," remarked the tall freedom fighter with green eyes.

All the farmers finished their wine and left the barn about five minutes after the resistant fighters made their exit. Pietro locked up the barn and made his way back to the house with Maria holding his hand. They entered the kitchen to see that only Anna and Catherina were sitting in a low, dim light of a lantern at the dining table. Maria ran to her mother's side to show her the candy that was given to her.

"Who gave you the candy?" asked Catherina.

"The man with green eyes said that I would have to share with my sister," replied Maria who was eating one of the pieces. Catherina took a deep breath and looked at her father, who was washing his hands in the sink.

"I am tired and have to start with the crops tomorrow, I am going to bed," Pietro said as he started his walk towards the bedroom without looking at his wife and daughter. Catherina hugged her daughter and started to cry as Anna gave her a hug as only a mother could.

* * *

Pietro walked into the barn the next morning knowing that the cow was his only way of getting the crops done unless he was going to do it himself, which would probably kill him. As he prepared the cow, he heard some noise in the front of the barn. It was Catherina and Anna coming in his direction; they both looked like they were ready for work.

"What do you two want?" asked Pietro.

"Shut up, old man, and let's get these fields done so we can rest up for the winter," replied Anna to her husband. Pietro smiled at his wife and daughter as they proceeded to help him the next couple of days getting the fields harvested and plant the winter crops.

The week went by very quickly and it was time for Pietro to make his trip to town to see what was going on with the auction house. The morning was very cold and probably was a good thing since everyone would be inside as Pietro rode his bike into town. Pietro turned into town from the main rode to see what was going on and if the auction house was open for business. Just as he approached, he noticed that the Germans were just about gone. Only a couple of sedans were left and the troop transporters were all gone. All the roadblocks were gone, but he did notice a sedan parked in front of Francisco's apartment, but that wasn't out of the ordinary. Pietro decided to take a chance and go talk with them. He noticed that the German soldiers were very young. As Pietro rode up to the German soldiers he handed them the hazelnuts from the basket of the bike. The German soldiers grabbed the nuts and looked at Pietro with a puzzled look.

"This is not an auction house anymore, old man. This is a way station for the labor camps. Would you like to go inside and see?" joked one of the soldiers.

Pietro backed away. "No, thank you. I must be getting on with my chores," answered Pietro who was moving the bicycle in the opposite direction of the soldiers. Pietro started his way out of town but didn't want to ride too quickly to attract attention. As he made his way out of the town, he heard the front gates open at the auction house. Pietro stopped just short of the turn towards the road heading out of town to see who or what was coming out. He noticed Francisco walking with two German soldiers towards a bus that was parked on the other side. Pietro concluded neither the Germans nor the Fascists would be raiding farms or insisting on crops. They were, essentially, abandoning the area. He continued his journey out of town without seeing anybody else.

***

The next morning, Pietro went outside with his coffee to look out over his empty fields that had been full of freshly cut crops the night before. He looked at the barn and noticed a black bag in the front, but nothing else that would have given an indication that someone was there that night to take his crops. Pietro walked over to the black bag and looked inside. He smiled as he walked back to the main house to share his good fortune with his family.

Chapter 21

CATHERINA ARRESTED

THE WEATHER HAD TURNED to the harsh bitter cold of winter with very little break from the sounds of war. Pietro was starting to worry that the Russians might come down from the northeast to rage revenge on Italy, which meant they would roll past this region on their way towards Mussolini's new headquarters in the north. The Russians were known to kill and rape in retaliation of the Axis Powers invasion of Russia. They did not care if you weren't in support of the invasion; you were of the right nationality for their revenge, which meant curtain death by very cruel methods. Pietro prayed for the Allies to finish their invasion of Italy and beat the Russian's to Berlin. Only time would tell, and Pietro was in a very difficult situation with no way of getting his family out the region. All he had were a couple of bikes and an old cow.

After the New Year, the rest of the German soldiers left the region and were replaced with Mussolini supporters—sketchy individuals. Francisco was making rounds, looking for people to send to the concentration camps. They would arrest family members for the slightest indication of Ally support or verbal outcry of the current Mussolini policies. They had visited the Zucchet farm several times but made no arrests since Chester and Bruno were already serving the Fuehrer in Germany.

Pietro stayed closer to the farm since the passing of the New Year, only visiting people late in the evening or meeting the other farmers at night. Pietro would not allow anybody to leave the farm for fear of being imprisoned. With so much going on in the region related to the war and imprisoning individuals, nobody came to inquire about Pietro's crop that he had harvested months ago. All the farmers bartered and all had more crops to keep for themselves since the Germans were no longing confiscating their food supplies. Still, the farmers were stressed from other problems plaguing this region, which were war related. Most of the farms in the region were shorthanded and left with only old men or women and children.

The sun rose from the east like it had every morning of Pietro's life. He was outside looking in its direction with his coffee in his hand and dressed with at least two layers of clothing. As he looked down, he noticed that his clothes were starting to show their wear. If fact, everybody needed new clothes, but until this war was over they would have to do with what was on the farm. He was very restless this morning and wondered what he was going to do that day. All his winter farming was done, thankfully. Even the gear was cleaned and stowed away for the spring season. The winter crops were the next big harvest, but that was another month away. His thoughts ran quickly back to the war as he heard the familiar sounds of bombing near the town and city areas. He knew that this war was just about over and that the Allies and Russians were going to win, but what he didn't know was when that was going to happen.

News about the war stopped months ago, and since he didn't go to town anymore, he was subject to only rumors of the farming community. What he did know was he hadn't heard anything from Chester or Bruno. The only contact he was having was with Gino but he hadn't been seen in months. Gino was on the run with the Alpine freedom fighters, working with the Allies to end this war. Pietro only prayed that they all would make it home after this war was over, but he knew better than to think all of them would come back—it was war and not everyone made it home.

As Pietro walked back to the main house after making his rounds of the farm, he noticed that there was a large dust ball in the distance. He opened the door, which led to the kitchen and yelled, "We may have some visitors. Anna, get everyone in their positions!" Pietro moved into his position in front of the main house to prepare for the possibility of visitors on this very cold morning.

Pietro waited patiently to see if what was coming his way was stopping at his farm. To his surprise the dust stopped just before his house and he looked to see that it was a bus full of people. Then a familiar sedan rolled into his driveway; it was Francisco's. Pietro knew this wasn't going to be a good visit. Francisco had at least six henchmen with him. Three were on the bus and three with him in the sedan. What Pietro noticed over the years was that Francisco got more courageous with more protection around him.

"How can we help you today, Herr Francisco?" asked Pietro as Francisco got out of the car with his henchmen.

"Where is Bruno Zucchet?" Pietro gave Francisco a puzzled look because Francisco knew that Bruno was working with the Germans and had not returned home in over a year.

"He is away with the other's, working with the Germans on the railroad. You know that, Francisco. He and the others haven't been home in over a year," answered Pietro as the henchmen went inside of the main house. Pietro looked in the house to see that everyone was in their place, but Anna was missing and probably in the kitchen.

"I want everyone out of the house!" yelled Francisco to the henchmen who had already escorted Catherina outside as she held Loretta and held Maria by the hand. Valarie and Velasco were right behind their sister. Anna was still inside and followed the henchmen up the stairs to check on Pietro's mother.

"Francisco, you know that Bruno hasn't been back in over a year. You know that. You were here when they came and took him," replied Pietro who was getting mad.

"According to my records, Bruno is not listed on the German roster that they supplied to me this week. So he is missing and needs to come with us or someone else will be coming with us today," Francisco demanded.

Anna emerged from the house and so did the other two henchmen. "There is no one else in the house except the old woman upstairs," replied one of the henchmen.

"Go check the rest of the farm and the barn," ordered Francisco. The henchmen did as they were told.

Anna looked at Pietro and asked, "Who are they looking for?"

Pietro looked at his wife and answered, "Bruno."

Anna looked at Francisco with a stern look like a mother would if their child had done something wrong. Francisco turned his attention towards the henchmen that were coming back from the barn area. Francisco couldn't look in Anna's direction. Anna grew up with Francisco's mother and they were very good friends until the war started.

"There is nobody else on this farm," replied one of the henchmen. Francisco stepped away from the main house with one of the henchmen who was carrying a pistol. They started to discuss something before they came back to Pietro.

Pietro was looking at Francisco's uniform while he was in his discussion with the henchmen and getting more agitated. *For the last five years this individual has caused nothing but aggravation to this family and farm*, Pietro thought.

Pietro knew that Francisco hadn't even been involved with any part of this war except to make this region his playground area, but that would end soon and Francisco would face a certain fate that he would not be able to find protection from.

"Mr. Zucchet, since we are unable to find Bruno, somebody will have to come with us until he is found or he turns himself into the authority," replied Francisco. Pietro was ready to lunge at Francisco when he felt his Anna grab his elbow. He turned to see her look deep into his eyes as if saying, *Please don't do this. We need you.*

Pietro took a deep breath and looked down at the ground and replied. "I will go with you."

Francisco took a step towards Pietro. "You are too old to work for the Germans."

"I will go with you. Just give me a minute to go get my stuff," answered Catherina. She handed Loretta to Pietro and Maria's hand to her mother.

Francisco made a hand gestured towards the bus for it to come to the drive way and pick up another passenger. As the bus got closer, Pietro and Anna noticed that it was full of war-aged females from the region.

The bus backed into the driveway and stopped just short of the main door. Pietro and Anna knew most of them; some of the women were yelling that they were kidnapped and that their families didn't know they were gone. Pietro walked over to Francisco to confront him. As he walked over to Francisco and the henchmen, they all turned away from the bus, which allowed Anna to quickly grab the notes before anybody noticed and promised all the girls that she would tell their families.

"Where are you taking everyone?" asked Pietro.

"That is none of your business," replied the henchman, who was noticeably bothered by Pietro's presence.

"Mr. Zucchet, you need to go back to the house or we will take you as well," replied Francisco.

Pietro already knew where they were going but wanted to distract them so Anna could get all the notes from the other passengers. As Pietro walked towards the house, Catherina was coming out of the house. Pietro noticed that she was wearing her traveling clothes and caring the only suitcase that the family owned. He began to tear up when he saw Maria start to cry for her mother to stay. Pietro approached his oldest daughter and grabbed her by her elbow with his free hand and whispered, "They are going to take you to the way station in town. You need to escape before the train arrives and takes you away. Do you understand me?"

Catherina looked into her father's eyes and replied, "I understand." She then reached for her eldest daughter in her father's arms to give her a hug goodbye. She then hugged her youngest daughter and her brother and sister as she made her way towards her mother. As she hugged Anna goodbye, Catherina could feel her mother start to cry and tremble in a way that she had not seen before. Anna spoke to her daughter very quickly before she was led towards the bus by one of the henchmen.

"Listen to your father and don't get on the train. We will tell him where they are taking you." Catherina kissed her mother and made her way onto the bus. She walked to the back of the bus so she could wave goodbye to what was left of her family.

Pietro was holding Maria and hugging his wife as the bus

pulled away from the farm. He could see Catherina wave to them from the back of the bus. Anna was very upset, as was Maria, Valarie, and Valasco. The only one not upset was Loretta, who was probably too young to understand what was happening.

"They will not be taking our daughter to any concentration camp as long as I am alive," Pietro said.

As the bus got smaller and eventually went out of sight of the farm Pietro spoke to everyone. "Let's all go inside and get something to eat."

Anna nodded her head in agreement as she helped with all the children. Just as all the remaining members of the Zucchet family entered the farmhouse, Pietro stopped just short of going into the house. He shut the door from the cold outside. Pietro walked towards the barn and looked towards the northern mountain range for some sign of activity. There was none. Pietro stood there staring and hoping that he would see the familiar light of hope. Nothing.

As the sun started its descent, the wind picked up, making it very cold for Pietro, who wasn't wearing his usual winter coat. He started to make his way back to the main house, but before he finished his usual walk, he turned to see if there was any light. Pietro began to shake as the cold was really starting to bother him, but just as he was turning, the light of hope came into his view. The signal meant that he would have visitors in his barn tonight.

The word must be out that the Fascists are arresting women, Pietro thought. *I wonder if Gino knows?*

***

After their evening meal, Pietro helped get the children ready for bed and then proceeded to the kitchen for his usual evening wine. Pietro kept looking out of the door of the kitchen to see if the barn door was left open, which was the signal that visitors had secretly arrived and were waiting for him.

"Is anyone here yet?" Anna asked.

Pietro nodded, finished his wine, and headed towards the door. "Keep everyone inside," he told his wife. "I have no idea who is there and whether it's more than one person. All I received was a signal that someone would be coming tonight."

Pietro could hear Anna start to cry. *The war is tearing this family apart. Three of our children are imprisoned by these ruthless Germans and Italian Fascists*, he thought. Pietro was going to make sure that his eldest daughter did not disappear without trying everything in his power to stop them from sending her to her certain death.

Pietro heard a noise from the back of the farm and knew it was his visitors that had finally arrived. He grabbed a couple bottles of wine before exiting the kitchen towards the open door barn.

Pietro entered the barn with hast, knowing that timing was of great importance. As he entered, Gino was standing there by himself with a look of desperation.

"Gino! I'm so glad you're here. I was hoping you would be. I have terrible news."

"Is it true? Did they take Catherina?" asked Gino.

"Yes, they did, and she is at the old auction house with about twenty other women from this area. Francisco arrested all of them for allegedly hiding all the railroad detail individuals but none of us has seen them since they left last year. What is going on?" asked Pietro as he handed the wine to his son-in-law.

"The Germans and Mussolini are in need of more laborers and are rounding up everybody they can to repair all the destruction of their countries, but it is too late. You don't have to worry about Catherina getting on a train, the tracks entering and leaving Cimpello and Pordenone are destroyed. I will make sure she is getting food, but it won't be long before this war is over."

Gino started to leave the barn. Pietro followed him out of the barn before they were seen by anyone. Gino made his way back to the mountains and Pietro returned back to the main house for some needed sleep.

Chapter 22

FEEDING THE HORSE

THE BUS HAD MADE two more stops after it left Pietro's. Both of the farms it inspected had been abandoned. Catherina was happy to see that no one else was arrested. The bus was about half full of all women, except for the bus driver and one guard. She knew about half the passengers on the bus and almost all were about her age. Catherina sat with her friend Julia, who she hadn't seen in over a year.

"What are you doing here, Julia?" asked Catherina to her childhood friend.

"I wish I knew. I was working in the fields when Francisco pulled up in his sedan and arrested me for hiding my brother. We haven't seen him since he left with Bruno over a year ago for the railroad work. What I am wearing is all I have. They didn't even take me home to get any clothes. My father and mother don't even know I am here, but I gave your mother a note for them."

"I packed some extra clothes, so we will be fine," Catherina said. "But we need to escape before we get on the train, Julia."

"How are we going to do that, Catherina?" Julia whispered.

"I don't know yet, but we both need to be strong and not show any weakness so you need to stop crying before they get mad at you," answered Catherina. Julia nodded, dabbing tears.

As the bus rolled into the town, Catherina could see that the streets were empty. She figured most people were either scared or there just wasn't anybody left to arrest and send to the labor camps. As Catherina looked out the window of the bus, she noticed that the bus stopped in front of the large gate on the side entrance of the old auction house. There were two Italian men with machine guns guarding the gate; neither of them had uniforms on but opened the gate when they saw the bus pull up. As the bus entered the converted way station, Catherina noticed that it was still the auction house but they had enclosed some of the open animal stalls into make-shift living quarters. There was still the open field with horses running around eating what grass was left, but there was no livestock.

The walls around the way station had been extended higher and broken glass was put in the cement on top to prevent people from escaping. The bus stopped just short of the entrance of the main building.

"Hold my hand and don't let go unless they force us to stop holding hands. Show no emotion, do what they tell us, and say nothing," said Catherina to Julia who looked terrified.

As they exited the bus, Catherina could see Francisco coming their way with the two henchmen on either side of him. There were guards everywhere and from the looks of them they were not friendly. Francisco stopped just short of the prisoners. He looked at Catherina with that smug look that turned her stomach.

"You will be housed here before you will be sent to your final destinations working in the labor camps. Each of you was arrested for hiding or being married to the Alpine freedom fighters who are enemies of our leader Mussolini," remarked Francisco.

"Where are you sending us," yelled one of the girls in the back. Francisco looked in her direction and waved at one of the guards. The guard grabbed the girl and took her to another section of the way station.

"Any more questions?" asked Francisco with the same smug look. After a minute of silence the guards started to lead the woman into the main building. Catherina and Julia continued to hold hands as they were led into the building.

The women were led into the main hall, which was converted into a large bunk room. There were bunks three high with most of them empty, which meant they must have just sent the last group on a train headed to Germany.

"Come on," whispered Catherina to Julia. Catherina led Julia to the back of the room, right next to one of the windows in the building. They set up right under the window in the bunks. If they could get through the window, they could escape through the horse field without being spotted. *It's the only way,* Catherina thought. Catherina took the top bunk so she could see outside.

***

Gino could see the auction house walls from the ridge that he was standing on just on the outskirts of Cimpello. He needed to get into town without being seen. He had a sack of food with him and some extra clothes provided by Pietro and Anna. If he could rescue Catherina they would need to go into hiding. Gino started his descent into town.

As Catherina laid her head down for the evening she heard the horses running, which was unusual late in the evening. She looked out the window and could see that someone was throwing food over the wall. The horses were running towards the wall to eat the food; they were just as hungry as everyone else. Catherina started to laugh a little knowing that someone was throwing food for the prisoners, but feeding the horses instead.

Chapter 23

Francisco Arrested

IT WAS THE END of March 1945 with no end in sight of
Catherina's captivity. It had been over two months since she had
arrived at the way station with little word about their departure
time. There were rumors that the railroad tracks were destroyed
on both sides of Cimpello and Pordenone, which made it
impossible to leave by train. But the prisoners could be hauled
by truck, bus, or, even worse, made to walk. The comforting
news was rumors that the Allies were defeating Germany's and
Italy's Fascists from all sides. Some speculated the war could
end in weeks.

Catherina and Julia stayed close during this period and were
able to get on the same work detail every day. They thought
about ways to escape through the window, but they had no way
to remove the bars.

Most of the work was conducted in the basement, which
was also sealed off. There they did laundry services for the
Fascists. Some of the women were sent to clean their barracks
or government buildings that the Fascists took over from the
Germans. But those work details were heavily guarded. There
were other women who had left the encampment and were
never seen again, like the boisterous girl who asked where they

were being sent on the first day they arrived. Others sent away didn't do what they were told or tried to escape.

Catherina and Julia were being closely watched by Francisco, which made it even more difficult to escape. Francisco assumed Gino was still alive and might try and rescue his wife. Pietro was also a clever old man who might try and orchestrate an escape. Catherina decided to play it safe and simply wait out the war.

Catherina and Julia would look out of their window at dusk to see if the food would be thrown over the wall. To their surprise, it would happen just about every day at the same time. Even the horses had started to walk over to the wall knowing the food would be coming. It started to be their only type of entertainment and a source of comfort knowing that someone cared so much that they would risk their lives to throw food for their loved ones.

Catherina and Julia were sitting next to their bunks having dinner and wondering when the bombings were going to start. Their dinners usually consisted of some bread and cheese that was given to them as they returned to their bunks after working all day.

"I wonder if we are going to see some flying food tonight?" asked Julia to Catherina who started to smile.

"I don't know, but I think the horses are heading in that direction," replied Catherina who started to get to her bunk to watch their evening entertainment.

As the evening came and went, there was no food thrown over the wall and even the horses seemed to be disappointed. As Catherina settled in for the evening, she laid her head down to go to sleep when she heard the familiar sounds of Ally bombing. Catherina got down from her bunk and took cover with Julia underneath the bunks until the bombings stop.

"Why is it that they only bomb just before we go to bed or when we are in the basement?" said Julia to Catherina as they both started to laugh. After about ten minutes the bombing stopped and they returned to their bunks for some well-needed sleep.

The next day started just like any other. Catherina and Julia headed to the basement to complete their tasks. But there were no guards in the basement, nor was there any laundry to be washed. It was just empty with the exception of the normal washing and cleaning gear lying around. Not even the head cleaning lady was available to give them orders.

"What should we do?" asked Julia to Catherina who was looking around the rest of the basement. "Let's head back up to see what the rest of the folks are doing," replied Catherina.

As they made their way to the main hallway, Catherina could see that all the rest of the women were gathered next to the windows looking through the bars. As they approached the crowd, Catherina asked the nearest girl, "What is going on?"

"We are locked up in here like cattle and they won't let us out to go home. We can see the guards, but they refuse to let us out of here. We heard that the Allies have defeated the Germans and Fascists and are headed this way."

Catherina made her way to the nearest window that looked out towards Francisco's main office. She looked for him in hopes that he would let them out. She could see a couple of Italians standing next to the office smoking cigarettes and holding machine guns, looking very nervous.

"Where is Francisco!" yelled Catherina. The guards looked in her direction but said nothing. "We are mothers, sisters, and daughters; don't let us die here. Unlock the doors and let us go!" yelled Catherina. The guards continued to ignore the women, not even giving a threatening glance.

"Please, let us out!" yelled another woman who was crying very loudly and pulling on the bars at the window in hopes for them to give way, but she was wasting her time. The inmates knew that the compound had been fortified by the Germans and would not be very easy to get out of without the doors being opened.

Catherina kept looking out of the window hoping to see someone approaching to free the prisoners, but the only people they saw were the two guards. She decided to look around the windows to see what was going on in the other parts of the compound. As she made her way to the other windows, she noticed that there was nobody to yell at and if there was a window in sight it was too far for them to hear her. She finally made her way back to her bunk to look out of the window, but just like the others, it was a waste of time. The area around the compound looked deserted. Even the horses were gone. That meant everyone was gone and they took the horses to get out of there. Catherina went back to the main doors in hopes of convincing Francisco to open them.

Francisco got up from his desk and headed towards the door. Just as he opened the door, he could hear all the prisoners yelling for his attention to let them go. He looked over in their direction for just a second before talking with his security detail.

"I just got a hold of the captain and he is sending us some more guards. The other ones were dispatched this morning to another part of the city. I am going to go see him and will be back this afternoon. Do not let anybody out of the building," ordered Francisco as he headed for his sedan. As one of the guards opened the main gate for Francisco, the women yelled for anyone's attention but there was nobody to hear their cries.

After Francisco drove off, the two guards started to yell at each other. Catherina couldn't hear what they were saying because of the noise the other prisoners were making, but she could tell from their body language that the exchange between the guards was heated. She watched as both guards headed to the main gate and left the compound. Just as they closed the gates, the prisoners heard gunfire. Now everyone was gone and there was no one to let the women out of the compound.

Catherina grabbed Julia by her arm and whispered, "Come with me back to the bunk room. We need to stay away from the main gate compound entrance in case they bomb this place."

Julia nodded and followed Catherina. Just as Catherina and Julia made their way towards the bunk room they could hear the planes approaching, but this time there was a lot of gunfire as well as the usual bombing noise.

Francisco could hear the bombing and gunfire too as he headed towards his apartment. This time it was closer than normal. He needed to get Betty and make his way up north. As he opened the door, Betty was standing there with two suitcases, waiting for him to get her.

"We need to move quickly and get out of here. I need to change my clothes before we go and then we will go out the side door," said Francisco as he started to take his uniform off for the last time. "The Allies are close. Most of our soldiers have fled."

"How are we going to get out of here?" asked Betty.

"I have another car parked in the back of the building that we are going to take," responded Francisco as he finished getting dressed. As he grabbed the suitcase he heard gunfire that was very close and decided to look out the window. Just as he looked outside, he could see unfamiliar uniforms rushing the main road heading towards the middle of town.

"We need to go now!" yelled Francisco as he grabbed Betty and headed out the door. As he headed down the stairs, he made the turn towards the side door just in time. He could hear the rush of troops coming down the road towards his apartment building. Francisco and Betty got inside the car and sped away in the opposite direction of their apartment building and the troops rushing his street. Francisco looked in his rearview mirror and saw nothing but old buildings of his past as he headed out of the town.

Francisco and Betty were just about to the next northern town thinking that they had escaped the Allies. Instead, he could see the roadblock ahead. Francisco slowed the car down so that they didn't look like they were trying to escape. As Francisco approached the roadblock, which also included a couple of tanks, he could tell that it was full of Ally and anti-Fascist Italian soldiers who were looking for anybody to arrest.

"Get out of the car!" yelled one of the soldiers. Francisco and Betty exited the car as ordered. "Where are your papers?" ordered the same soldier who was holding a machine gun. Francisco grabbed the forged papers from the breast pocket of his jacket that he had made long ago just in case something like this would happen. He handed the papers to the soldiers.

"Nice boots!" one of the soldiers said. "You don't look like a farmer to me." Then the soldier grabbed the bottom of his right pant leg and pulled it up to reveal his shinny boots. Betty looked down and noticed that Francisco didn't change his shoes when he changed his clothes. Francisco smiled at him and then noticed some villagers coming from behind the tank.

Chapter 24

CATHERINA RETURNS

THERE WAS SHOOTING ON the outside walls of the way station that lasted for about forty-five minutes. Catherina and Julia were still in the bunk room when the shooting stopped and then they heard troops moving away from the compound. Catherina was looking out of the window when Julia asked, "What do you see?"

"I see a lot of smoke but that is all," replied Catherina. Then Catherina got down from the bunk. "I see planes coming this way, we need to take cover under the bunks." The sound of descending bombs made the screaming noise that Catherina had learned to hate and fear. The ground started to shake as the bombs roared into the ground exploded as they hit. Then the whole compound started to shake as the bombs got closer. One hit just outside the way station, exploding a section of the compound wall. The walls of the bunk room started to crumble around Catherina and Julia. The front door area facing the courtyard was hit. Most of the other prisoners were either in that area or the basement when the bombs hit.

Pietro could see the planes dropping bombs on the town and felt helpless. He knew, based on what Gino had reported that Catherina was still likely there. If he left the farm, then the whole family was in jeopardy of being harmed. So, he had to wait and hope. His place was at the farm with his wife, children, and grandchildren. He was bound to ensure their safety was his priority.

The bombing lasted for only for a few minutes, but the devastation was immense.

"Are you alright?" asked Catherina to Julia who was kneeling next to her.

"Yes, I am fine. The bunks saved us," replied Julia.

"Let's get out of here before they start bombing again," replied Catherina.

Catherina and Julia dug their way out from under the bunk after they felt that the bombing had stopped. All they could hear was screaming coming from what was left of the front door area and basement. As they made their way towards the other prisoners to help them, Catherina could see that the way station was in ruins. Francisco's office was totally gone and so were most of the walls that kept them in this horrible place. As they began working to remove the rocks and debris, Catherina noticed that there were already other people from the town helping out. She had not seen this many people out and about in more than six months.

As nightfall got closer, the Ally soldiers entered the city but they didn't stop to help. They were on their way to Germany to end this war. One by one the women prisoners were removed from the debris. Most survived with only minor injuries, but a few didn't make it through the bombing. Catherina learned days later that the Allies were convinced that this was a barracks for the German and Fascist soldiers. Catherina and Julia helped throughout the next morning, but then they had to get back home.

* * *

Pietro was up early the next morning looking out of the kitchen window and could still see the smoke coming from town. He was getting worried and decided that he was going to town today. The Ally soldiers and tanks had already gone by yesterday and bombings had stopped, so he would have to take a chance today. Just as he was finishing his coffee, he felt a tug on his pants. He looked down and it was Maria. "Nono, can I go outside and play?" asked his oldest granddaughter.

Pietro kneeled down to look at his granddaughter and said, "Yes, you can, but you must stay in the driveway and don't go past the end. If you see anybody coming down the road you need to come back inside the house and tell me." Before he could finish talking to Maria she was already heading out the door excited that she was able to go outside without anyone supervising. Pietro could see her go down to the end of the driveway towards the rock pile. She always enjoyed climbing on it and throwing rocks into the field.

Maria was busy gathering her pile of rocks and didn't notice the person running towards her from the fields. As she started to throw her first rock, she looked up towards the fields and noticed someone coming towards her with their arms opened. Maria dropped her rock and started to run back towards the house.

"Nono, someone is running and yelling at me!" Pietro looked very concerned at first and started to wave at Maria to run towards his direction. Maria jumped into her Nono's arms and at the same time he picked her up. Pietro looked at the figure running toward the house. He gave his granddaughter a tight hug and smiled.

"No need to be afraid, little one," he said. "That's your momma . . . Anna you need to come outside, Catherina is home!"

Maria turned her head to see her mother running down the driveway yelling, "Maria, it is me, your mother!"

Chapter 25

ALLIES TAKE OVER

IT HAD BEEN A week since Catherina had escaped and the Allies marched through the region. The bombings and shootings had stopped since Catherina returned home. Pietro had made a trip back to town after a couple of days and came back with the latest news that the war was almost over and Mussolini was on the run. The Allies had run off the Fascist supporters. For the first time in over seven years the area was not under their control.

It was Saturday and Catherina wanted to go to town. She wanted to see how everyone was doing that was hurt during the bombing. Besides, she needed to do some shopping. As she made her way to the barn to get her bike, Maria was right behind.

"Mom, can I come with you, please?" asked Maria. Maria hadn't been to town in over a year. Catherina felt somewhat guilty that she was gone for so long.

She replied. "Yes, you can come with me. Let me get you on the handle bars after we get on the main road." Maria started to scream that she was going to town with her mother. It was a very nice day so heavy jackets were not going to be needed. Besides, Catherina wasn't going to stay in town too long. Catherina let Anna know that Maria was going with her as she made her way to the main road with her oldest daughter next to her and the bike.

As Catherina made her way towards town, she could see that there were lots of people coming and going to town. She had not seen this in a very long time, but she noticed that some of the people leaving town had somewhat of a disturbed look on their faces. Catherina made the last turn towards the market place and stopped her bike as she noticed what was causing the looks on their face. She could see three separate ropes hanging down from the train overpass. At the end of the ropes were three men that were hanging from their necks. To the right of the hung men were a group of women that had their hands tied together and were being marched through town by one common rope. Each of the women had their heads saved and wore prisoner's uniforms, the same type that Catherina wore while detained at the way station. Most of the people in town were throwing rocks or food at the women. Catherina noticed that the first one being paraded through town was Betty. The rest were German or Fascist supporters, many of whom had been openly abusive to the locals during the last years of the war. Catherina looked back towards the men hanging from the overpass and noticed the middle one was wearing very shiny boots, which she had seen so many times over the years.

Maria was startled and looked at her mom and asked, "Mom, can we go home?" Catherina turned her bike around and headed out of town knowing that justice had been served.

***

The farm only had a few chickens and one cow at the end of the war but would soon become a very productive farm as it was before the war. Chester and Bruno would make their way back home from Germany, but unfortunately Bruno's health was falling at a rapid rate when he finally made it home. He would not last the year before he passed away from the tortures of war and Tuberculosis.

As for Gino, he finally made it home months after the war had ended. He tried many times to rescue Catherina from the way station but feared for her safety and the others. Their unit did not have the proper armament to rescue the people held in the way station, which was heavily guarded. His unit left the Cimpello region to fight the retreating Germans just days before the bombing of the way station. He did not find out what happened to Catherina until he returned from fighting the enemy. During the latter part of the war, he wanted to return to the farm and be with his family but feared for their safety, so he stayed away. The families that were caught hiding deserters were imprisoned or put to death. What he witnessed during the war haunted him for the rest of his life and he would never recover from his nightmares. At the end of the war, only his mother survived.

Epilogue

AS A YOUNG BOY and throughout my teenage years, my family would spend countless days visiting and living with all my family members in Cimpello and Prodenone. Gino and Catherina were the perfect grandparents that always showered us with small gifts and spent all of their time with us when we were visiting or when they came to stay with our family. They never spoke of the war when it was just our immediate family, but when the extended families would meet at the Zucchet farm it was a different story. It was when the wine and food appeared that the old stories became new again. The Germans and Mussolini were always the major topic with Catherina, Chester, Valeria, and Valasco. I can never remember my grandfather talking about the war when family was around, but he would always seem to withdraw from the conversation when anyone would bring the war up. He would, however, drink wine until it was gone or he had to go to bed. My grandfather would spend a lot of time with me in the basement of his modest apartment that he shared with my grandmother, Catherina. It was there that he would talk to me about life and care for the birds that he had caged as pets, always feeding them and talking to them as if they were family members. He would occasionally fall silent and sit with his wine staring out of the lone window catching the memories of his past. Sometimes he did drift to the war years and briefly mention his times, but only in humor, and he would only briefly talk about the horrors of the war.

There are moments of my childhood and teenage years that stand out when we spent time with my grandfather. One would be that he would always take my brother and me to the local watering holes to show off his grandsons. He would always sit at the bar while we would be in the game room next to the bar. What he didn't know was that I would listen for hours about his war experience that he would share with his war friends. It was only years later while I was in the navy that I understood why he would let go with his war friends and not his immediate family. The one memory that made the biggest impact on me was what happened one day at the beach in Italy. My grandfather took the whole family to the beach on the perfect beach day. Then, as I sat next to my grandfather having lunch, he suddenly got very angry and left the beach to sit in the car. This puzzled me so I went to talk with him and found out that some German tourist had sat next to us on the beach. Gino would always carry a hatred for the Germans well into his sixties.

Years later, when my father was stationed in Germany, Gino would come, and in the beginning he would avoid all contact with Germans. He would even stay in the house when we would venture out to local towns for a meal. Although, during his last visit with us in Germany, he did join us for an outing and seemed to have made peace with the enemy that gave him so much pain during his lifetime.

I visited my grandmother several times during my 20s, but by then my grandfather had passed away. Even though my Italian wasn't as good as it was when I was younger, we still could communicate and have a great time. We would visit the farm and Chester, Valerie, and Valsco would join us with all of their families. What a great time we would have, and I still think there was no other place where the food and wine tasted so good. During my many visits, she would get on her bike and ride twelve miles a day to visit my grandfather and lay flowers on his grave. It was the most moving thing I have ever seen. She did this well into her eighties.

Maria and Loretta left for America in their late teens and have been married to my father and uncle for over fifty years. It is a wonder to see my mother and aunt together, going back and forth as they use Italian and English with an ease that most Americans can only watch in disbelief. As their children grew up and started their own lives, they seemed to grow closer and would often talk about their time on the farm during those hard times. While I was writing this book and interviewing them, I could see their eyes and facial expressions shift into a distant trance as they spoke of their time on the farm. My heart would always sink a little as they remembered those years and their eyes would water. I could not help but to see their pain. It was the hardest of times, but through the love of family and the courage of the Zucchet and Cartelli families they survived the brutality of many. Today the farm is only a mirror of what it was back during the war. All of my family members that endured such hardship during the war have all but passed away, but their legacy will live for generations to come.

If you enjoyed this book, look for the continuation book that follows Gino Cartelli and his exploits as the Italian freedom fighter.

Bruno Zucchet,
before the war.

[handwritten note, partially legible:] Mio caro Bu...
man... il 12-1-45
...o mesi di luna...
...ta...
...

Gino Cartelli
in 1939.

Catherine Zucchet.

Loretta Cartelli in front of the main house. Notice the water pump to her left and one of the hidden pots on her right that they unearthed after the war.

Maria and Loretta as teenagers.

Maria Cartelli in the
planting fields in front of
the farm 1945.

Pietro Zucchet in his
barn with the cow in
the background. Picture
taken 1945.

Pietro Zucchet's World
War I picture.

Zucchet family 1928.

Picture taken the day after the war was over.

CPSIA information can be obtained at www.ICGtesting.com
Printed in the USA
BVOW08*0318100616

451478BV00019B/10/P

9 781633 933156